DAPHNE GLAZER

DAPHNE GLAZER was born in Sheffield and now lives in Hull. She spent five years in Nigeria teaching German to adults, and on her return to England had a spell making toffees in a factory, taught in a maximum security prison and a borstal, and is now a lecturer at Hull College of Further Education.

Her stories have appeared in magazines such as *New Statesman and Society*, *Critical Quarterly* and *Panurge* and have been featured on Radio 4's *Morning Story*. She is the author of a novel, THREE WOMEN, published in 1984.

The Last Oasis

DAPHNE GLAZER

THE SUMACH PRESS

First published in Great Britain 1992 by
The Sumach Press
29 Mount Pleasant, St Albans, Herts AL3 4QY

BRITISH LIBRARY CATALOGUING IN PUBLICATION DATA

Glazer, Daphne
The last oasis
I. Title
823 (F)

ISBN 0-7126-5264-7

Photoset in Linotron Baskerville by
Rowland Phototypesetting Limited
Bury St Edmunds, Suffolk
Printed and bound in Great Britain by
Mackays of Chatham plc, Chatham, Kent

ACKNOWLEDGEMENTS

Out of the Dragon's Mouth, *Got The Message*, *The Loss* and *Destiny Waltz* first appeared on B.B.C. Radio 4 Morning Story. *Love's Coming of Age* was included in an Iron Women Anthology.

For Peter Imo and Sebastian who listened
and Heather who pointed the way.

CONTENTS

Business Before Pleasure

IT WAS WINNING the 'Dream Holiday for Two' that did it. Like the forbidden fruit in the Garden of Eden it changed things for ever.

Me and Jason'll be able to go, she'd told her mother. Eh, think about it . . . Bermuda . . . it'll be like that Bacardi Coke ad . . . rafts and palm trees and surf! Beautiful people, she'd thought, and cut-away swimsuits.

Joanne had decided she'd phone Jason from work and tell him.

All the way down the village street, she'd wafted along to the bus stop. The damp October day promised all manner of tantalizing possibilities.

Jason might be in the farm office or out at the butchery . . . wherever, she'd catch him.

The hour's bus ride into town to work hadn't dragged. She'd not wanted anyone to speak to her, because she was planning her wardrobe: a new swimsuit . . . black, perhaps, with a vivid stripe . . . several suntops . . . strapless sundresses for long hot evenings where you sipped Bacardi Coke from tall frosted glasses and listened to the surf breaking. There would be dancing on a terrace. And then the bedroom scene . . . a white satin négligé . . . In films heroines always had that carefully arranged, slightly dishevelled, pouty look. Their négligés would droop off one shoulder and they would pose by french windows to stare out at the bay in the moonlight. Their lovers would appear and stick frangipani blossoms in their hair and sweep them off to bed. The bed would have loose, gauzy drapes . . .

It would be a sort of honeymoon. Joanne had never been

out of the country and rarely out of the village – except for work and occasional holidays to Blackpool. Now, suddenly the village and everything about it seemed too small. Everybody lived in everybody else's pocket.

The news had bubbled inside her – she couldn't wait to tell him. She'd rushed across the college concourse and up the steps, through the swing-doors and into the lift – all in one bound of anticipation. The boss hadn't arrived. Good. Then she'd been dialling and waiting. Mrs Brennan had answered.

Oh, Joanne, hello, love . . . bit early for you.

I'm at work.

Anything wrong?

No . . . Please could I have a little word with Jason?

Just a minute, we're very busy.

Joanne had pictured Mrs Brennan with her auburn blow-waved hair that had an acrylic gleam and her scarlet nails and knuckle-duster rings. They made her hands into claws that patted and counted.

Joanne, what's up?

Jay, fantastic news . . . I've won a holiday for two . . .

Silence . . . and then Oh . . . Just, oh, like that, and Got to go, very busy . . . See you later.

She'd not been able to believe it. He'd dismissed it all. The word processor had squatted there waiting for her, and the piles of student references. Soon the bilious-green letters had winked up on the screen.

Barry Maws shows considerable linguistic ability . . .

Amanda Smedley cannot formulate a logical argument and has difficulty . . .

On, on, all day until five o'clock and then her head was pounding.

The journey back home on the bus scratched her nerves. Two women behind her talked sudden deaths. Well, I saw him last week, and then on Monday he were dead . . .

Some college kids swapped gossip, and the bus engine droned; the windows were covered with a tissue-paper film.

Out there white sandy beaches shadowed by palm trees waited . . .

Up High Street she plonked, scowling in her secretary's court shoes and her neat black mac. Why should it be called 'High Street', this street out in the country? She saw Mrs Fletcher from the post office, just leaving.

'Hello, Joanne, how are you, love – look a bit down in the mouth! Busy day?'

'Oh, yes, Mrs Fletcher . . . very busy.'

Mrs Fletcher had been one of the first to congratulate her on her engagement, she remembered.

You've done well, love, haven't you? I mean, Jason's mum and dad aren't short, are they?

Brennans had the biggest farm around and the butchery business. Jason was their only son.

Yes, done very well, you have, love . . .

Mr and Mrs Brennan didn't agree. Joanne's dad was a tenant farmer and that didn't amount to much.

Well, of course, your dad . . . he's not a proper farmer as such, is he? Mrs Brennan had been clopping about on the ceramic tiles in the big kitchen, popping stainless-steel pans on the Aga. They always ate very elaborately at Brennans': meat every day – often best steak – creamy mashed potatoes, broccoli in white sauce. Mrs Brennan had two women in to help – one for cleaning and general work and the other to assist with the cooking. She'd invariably drop out these devastating sentences whilst she was peering into a pan, or consulting a cookery book. It was amazing the poison didn't affect the cooking. Joanne had never known what to say.

Jason turned up at eight-thirty. They were to go for a drink at the Coach and Horses. The pubs were the only places for an evening out and they were packed with people in their teens or early twenties and elderly men. Once you'd got married, you stayed at home and watched telly.

'What do you want, Jo? Usual?'

'No,' she said suddenly. 'I'd like something a bit different for a change – a Bacardi Coke, please.'

'What for?'

'Because I feel like it.'

Half of lager, half of lager . . . she was tired of it; tired of the pattern of the words.

She watched him approaching the bar. The discreet lighting shone on his black leather bomber jacket and his black, slicked-back hair. He was very precise about his dress, and his things had to be spotless. Mrs Brennan was the same: carved auburn waves, blue wings above her eyes, black mascara, a scarlet or plum-red mouth – and the rings. The rings were always there. Did she sleep in them?

Mr Brennan was very smart too. He'd wear a navy-blue blazer and grey flannels and a navy-blue tie and his cheeks were like bleeding steak, and when you stood near him, you could see that the redness was composed of thousands of little scarlet thread-veins. He had big square reddish hands and his wedding-ring was thick and yellow.

Two girls at the bar turned to stare at Jason. Joanne saw them twittering at each other and exchanging banter with him. Jason had a dark, shiny beauty, that was why she'd fallen for him. She'd met him at a Christmas party and at the time they'd both been engaged to someone else. When he'd looked at her, that had been that . . .

Hello, he'd said, what's your name?

She'd liked the blue shadows down his cheeks and his pewter-coloured skin and his very red lips and his boxer's build. All around them party poppers had been snapping and kids were laughing and draping each other with the thin baby-blue and pink streamers, and he'd wound them round her shoulders and she'd been somehow shocked by that. It had been as though he was doing something very intimate.

The next day he'd phoned her at home.

Joanne, he'd said, this is Jason Brennan here. Could I take you for a drink?

Nothing subsequently had been quite like that first evening, their meeting at the party.

I want to get engaged, he'd said, not long afterwards. I want to buy you a ring.

She'd wondered about that – engagements seemed unlucky; no sooner were you engaged than the magic disappeared – but she'd said yes.

He'd had to ask his parents for the money.

Oh, they don't pay me, he'd said, I just have to ask if I want anything – everything has to be ploughed back into the business.

She hadn't liked the idea of her ruby and diamond ring coming from Mrs Brennan . . .

'Here you are, Jo,' he said, handing her the glass of Bacardi Coke.

'You've not said a thing about my good news,' she said.

'Oh yes – what was it all about then?'

She told him.

'It's the chance of a lifetime and we don't have to pay anything – all found – can you imagine, Jay?'

He listened and sipped his pint. Joanne waited, letting her eyes wander over the girls at the bar in their mini-skirts and shiny blouses; big gold hoops shone in their ears and their nails were glossy red. She never wore thigh-high skirts even though a lot of her age group did. Her skirts fell nearly to her ankles and covered her black boots. She didn't want to be all on display like a prize Friesian.

'I don't think I'll be able to get.'

She heard his flat voice and looked down at his square hands – he had his father's hands, she registered. They spent days slicing up joints, because he was in charge of the butchery. Once she'd gone there to help for a week, even taken her annual holiday, because they'd been short-staffed, and she'd seen him wielding a shiny cleaver to hack at a lamb carcass which was hanging up on skewers. She'd watched the way the blade scythed through the white bone and red flesh and the suspended carcass split down the middle obscenely. He'd cut joints of pork and beef very precisely, shaping the flesh between his fingers, paring away a hunk of fat, forming a neat square and talking to the customers –

Yes, you'll like that – not a bit of fat on it . . .

He wore a white overall and a blue and white striped apron at work and she'd noticed how the apron became splattered with blood and the shop had a peculiar heavy, acidic smell – it was the blood, she supposed, and all those trays of chops and sides of beef and chains of sausages and the yellow-skinned poultry and the maroon-coloured slabs of liver in white enamel dishes, and she'd felt a bit sick.

One of the reasons she'd never wanted to have anything to do with farming as a career had been perhaps because of this dislike of turning animals into food. No, she'd known from being a little kid that she wanted to be a secretary and type letters and use word processors and computers – things that had nothing to do with farming . . . you couldn't hurt them and they were grey and clean and could be wiped down and made no mess.

'What's the matter?'

'Why don't you think you can go? Your parents wouldn't have to pay anything.'

'They won't be able to spare me.'

She remembered the precision of his hand wielding the cleaver.

'They might.'

'I doubt it.'

'Oh, Jason, for goodness' sake! They don't let you have a life. We hardly get out together at all.'

'It's the business.'

'But there's more to life than business.'

She hadn't known she was so angry. Her heart was donging like a gong and she felt a wave of heat engulfing her chest.

'I can't leave 'em in the lurch.'

'Just for two weeks – it's not two years.'

'Well, I'll try, but I bet they say no.'

'Jason, we're twenty-one! We're not kids.'

He walked her home from the pub in the mysterious foggy

night. In the fields the dark shapes of cattle shifted. Joanne listened to her boots ringing on the road. The trees stood motionless. The sycamores had great yellow tattery leaves, like bunches of bananas. Now and then a leaf would tumble down, causing a dry, scratchy sound that made Joanne shudder.

She heard Mrs Brennan's voice:

Oh, hello, Joanne, nice to see you . . . Haven't you got another jumper, dear? You always seem to be wearing that one.

'I'll ask 'em when I get in,' he said.

'All right.' She had nothing more to say. He was holding her hand, interlacing his fingers in hers, and the thrill shot right up her arm like an electric charge, but she was still angry. Something scrabbled in the hedgerow. A dog barked. Fog swirled, sucked them in as though into a cave. They stopped by the roadside and kissed. His warm, moist mouth pressed blindly against her cheek, found her lips. They swayed against the hedge.

'You see, if we went away on our own, we could do anything we liked.'

He pulled away. 'Yes,' he said, but she thought there was a coldness in his voice.

The next day she rang him after work. He was working late, Mrs Brennan said. Yes, she would tell him that Joanne had rung, when he appeared.

Joanne washed two blouses and ironed a shirt, all in a suppressed fury. Her mother had gone to the Women's Guild and her dad was at the pub.

It was ten before Jason phoned back.

'I've been that busy, Jo, couldn't phone before.'

'Oh. Well?'

'Well what?'

'Did you ask?'

'Yes, but it's no good – can't.'

Can't . . . can't . . . She thought of the raft floating way out on the still, warm water. Palm fronds rustled in the breeze and cast black splodges of shadow on white sand. And he was throwing it all away for the carcasses that thumped dully on the counters; the white chest freezers gasping with coldness when they were opened for a moment. Mrs Brennan's favourite word was 'business', 'the business':

We've built up the business from scratch, you know, Joanne. *We* believe in hard work. It gets its own reward, hard work . . .

'Oh,' Joanne heard herself say. 'Oh, I see . . . Well, see you, then.'

'Joanne?'

'Yes?'

'See you Saturday . . .'

'I'm not sure.'

'What do you mean?'

'I might be doing something . . . Well, bye now.'

She hung up and then sat concentrating on the bounding of her heart. If she didn't act now, they'd carry on like they had been doing and it would be the same year after year: pub once or twice a week if they were lucky – a dinner-dance every blue moon or somebody's wedding or engagement party – but that was never sure. And always the business and Mrs Brennan:

Oh, hello, Joanne, how are you? You'd look better if you wore a nice bright colour and a bit of make-up. You're too pale, you know – not enough colour . . .

She didn't see him that weekend, and on the Monday when she arrived home from work she said to her mother, who had just come back from the Mothers' Union meeting in the village hall, 'Mum, I want to go into a flat with Tricia, one of the secretaries at College – she's looking for a flatmate.'

'You do right, love . . . but what about Jason then?'

'I don't want to be sitting round waiting for him all my life.'

She saw Jason once before the move. They sat in the pub at their usual table in the corner.

'If you go,' he said, 'that's it.'

'All right,' she said, gulping down her Bacardi Coke.

He didn't speak again. She kept glimpsing his hands holding his beer glass or fiddling with a beer mat. Black hair grew on their backs.

You're sentimental, he'd once told her. Meat's meat . . . Your dad farms . . . Everybody who farms knows how it is – it's only townies who see meat in Sainsbury's in cellophane packages that start bleating . . .

'Well,' he said, 'I suppose we'd best be getting back.'

'Yes, I suppose so.'

In silence they walked down the road. It was splattered with yellow sycamore leaves now and they lay like splayed hands on the shiny blackness.

It's all over, she thought, all over – but somehow she couldn't bear the idea of never seeing him again. Inside her churned anger and despair and still the old attraction, because she couldn't escape it. She liked his deep-blue eyes and black lashes and his shiny black hair. His butcher's hands charmed and revolted her. But there was this other side: the obsessive worker, the one who lived for business, who had a scrubbed smartness – a Mrs Brennan smartness. His bomber jacket shone, just like his leather casuals and the heavy gold bracelet on his Rolex watch, his twenty-first present from his mother. His family were buying up acres, expanding, extending the butchery:

We believe in hard work . . .

If he could have escaped, he would have been different . . . But could he? Had it ever entered his head? Would he kiss her at the gate; come in; walk away?

'So you've decided then?'

'Yes . . . I want to get away from here – it's suffocating – I want to lead my own life.'

He was white in the face and that was unusual, and his eyes looked hard and black in that light.

'Goodbye then.'

Yes, she thought, his mother's won – they've got him body and soul . . . he'll never, ever escape.

He turned and walked off. He swung his shoulders. Even

without seeing him, she knew how he looked and a sickness came over her. He'd gone . . . It was all over.

She moved into the flat on a Saturday. Her flatmate, Tricia, was away at the time, gone home for the weekend. So there she was, alone for the first time in her entire life. It was a strange feeling.

After she'd closed the curtains, turned on the telly and settled herself with a mug of coffee and a plate of biscuits some of the oddness seemed to disappear. It was all slightly unreal, as though she had now assumed responsibility for herself: she would have to turn out the lights, snap off the gas fire, decide when it was bedtime – she would have to be the one who listened for prowlers and unusual sounds . . . she must act. There was nothing to protect her from what would come . . . no comfortable buffer between her and the Bermuda breakers . . .

Little shivers of panic prickled down her back and shoulders but she sipped her coffee and gazed resolutely at the screen. Then the doorbell pinged. All of a sudden she was terrified. There seemed to be acres of room and the silence was deeper because the doorbell had broken it. Should she pretend she hadn't heard? She got up and went into the corridor, her heart blundering and bounding with fear.

She eased the door open on the chain. Jason was standing there, his cheeks red, his eyes bright.

'Jo,' he said, 'I've come to see you.'

'Oh, right . . .'

'You don't mind?'

'Of course not . . . come in.' She unchained the door and went through all the motions in a dream. He took off his leather jacket and draped it on the back of a chair and sat there in his white shirt, which was open at the neck so that she glimpsed the dark hair which lay like fur on his chest. The hair seemed impossibly erotic – animal and male . . . she thought of bulls with chocolate-brown curly hair; of shaggy Highland cattle with long fringes trailing in their eyes; pelts . . . foxes . . . Under the thin cotton she could make out the dark pips of his small hard nipples and that too caused the excitement to flutter in her throat. They had never been alone like this before – there had always been his mother hovering, or his parents watching telly or at least never far away. And now, here they were in this room on a Saturday evening . . . everything was pending . . .

'Do you want a coffee?'

He said yes and she went through into the kitchenette. She felt she was different in that place . . . and he was too. It was like playing at house . . . she'd done that as a little girl. Now I'm the Mummy and I'm making the dinner and you . . .

If she'd met him for the first time now, she wouldn't have known anything about the butchering or Mrs Brennan and her copper waves and her rings and her bright red nails. He'd just have been a man with red cheeks and blue eyes and glassy black hair. They were out drifting on a raft under a melon moon and the air was filled with the drone of cicadas . . .

'Thanks,' he said as she handed him the coffee, and he sat there on the sofa with his thighs spread wide and his hands braced round the mug, and she gave a secret shudder which started in her stomach like pins and needles and became a thrill.

'Flat looks all right.'

'Yes, it's real comfortable . . . won't be hard to clean either. Tricia's at her mum and dad's this weekend – back tomorrow night. How've you been?'

'All right. Got a lot on.'

He talked, she listened. She stared at his hands and avoided prolonged eye-contact.

It got to eleven o'clock, midnight . . .

'I'd best push off.'

'Yes,' she said. 'Does your mother know where you are?'

'No.'

'Well then . . .'

She waited. The evening had drawn into that moment. She studied her fingernails.

'It's a pity . . .' he began, and was staring at her.

'Yes?'

'That we live that far away.'

'You could stay the night.' She felt the blood whoosh into her cheeks.

He hesitated for the merest moment.

'Right,' he said, 'right . . . yer . . .'

They stood up at the same time. She kept glancing at the fur in the neck of his shirt and she seemed to feel inside her the awful glancing of the cleaver striking through flesh and bone . . . There was something blunted, yet powerful, about him; things she couldn't understand. He kissed her then.

'You go and get into bed,' he said, 'I'll just use your loo.'

'Right.'

This was some strange dream; something she hadn't expected; she'd never dreamt he'd come. His mother wouldn't have allowed it. Brennans didn't let go like that.

She took off her sweater and skirt and sprayed a mist of Poison (his last Christmas present to her) over her neck and at her armpits. Naked she lay under the duvet and waited.

She didn't look at him as he slipped off his clothes. Just as he was about to slide in beside her, she heard the phone start ringing.

'I'd better answer it . . . oh God!'

She felt stupid, winding herself into her towelling dressing-gown and racing into the sitting room.

A man's voice spoke to her. 'Is that you, Joanne?'

'Yes,' she said, and the icy goose-pimples rose on her back.

'It's Mr Brennan here. Is our Jason with you?'

'Yes,' she said.

'Mrs Brennan's been took ill – we've had to get the doctor . . . Get him, will you!'

'Yes.'

She returned to the bedroom. 'Jason, it's your dad.'

Something changed in his face. It went hard and different. She hovered near him as he talked into the mouthpiece.

'Yes,' he kept repeating, 'yes.'

'Well?'

'I'll have to go home,' he said, 'she's ill . . . very bad, my dad said.'

'Never mind,' Joanne said, 'perhaps another time . . .' But she knew that Mrs Brennan would see that there never was another time.

Out of the Dragon's Mouth

On this morning when Ivy had been cleaning the glass tooth for thirty years, that nasty little woman, Whitney, had called her in.

'Mrs Smedley, I don't like to have to say this . . . no, I really don't, but I have no option . . .' And she'd drawn herself up real tall. She was only the supervisor, after all, but you'd think she'd been born in her little suit and stilettos, toting her shiny executive case.

Anyway, she'd been speaking for about ten minutes before Ivy had understood what she was on about.

'. . . so you being the age you are . . . I'm having to suggest that you retire.'

Retire! She went boiling hot and her heart fluttered at the word. Why, she'd come there cleaning when the kiddies were little. Her mother-in-law had suggested it.

'Look there, Ivy, they've opened that big new college – go over and ask 'em if they'd take you on. It 'ud be a nice little job, like. You could fit it in dead easy while the kiddies are small. It wouldn't be for long like.'

And she had done – first thing in a morning at six o'clock she'd be fettling away; back again at four-thirty till six-thirty.

It had started off as her helping to supplement Ron's wage, and then Ron had run off with the receptionist at his garage. So, there she'd been, on her own with her three.

She'd seen cleaners come and cleaners go, but there'd always been Marge, her friend, who was on floor five when she was on four. They'd brewed up at eight in one of the classrooms on her floor, and Billy and George, the two caretakers, would drop in for a cuppa as well, bringing the tea-bags they'd dried out on the radiator. They'd have a good groan about council rents, and Billy would complain about his mother, and George about 'our lass', his wife. And it had seemed that they might carry on like this for ever: bairns got married and had bairns; principals came and went; nameplates changed on doors; walls were painted; it was always freezing at the front when the west wind blasted in from the estuary, and roasting when sun shone. But she had to say it, she had begun to notice how, like her, that eight-storey glass tooth had started to fall apart. First it had been the great black gobs of tar which had started raining down on the seventh floor; then the window-frames had gone rotten. The doors in the foyer had smashed when there was a gale. The doors in the girls' lavs wouldn't fasten. The drinking-fountain puddled all over the toilets. Somebody had been poisoned by drinking water from the taps. There had been all sorts of rumours about dead things in the water-tanks.

As she'd watched everything gradually growing more battered, she'd felt how her back gave her twinges and noticed how her face was suet-coloured and her hair turning grey. Mind you, nobody knew that, because she'd been putting lightener on it for years.

So when that nasty Whitney gave her her cards, it had seemed like the end.

Marge and George and Billy had gathered round her at tea-time.

'Oh, she's a rotten bit o' work!' Billy had rumbled through his flappy lips. He never bothered to wear his dentures, said he couldn't master 'em.

'Too bad, lass,' George said, 'bad luck, love . . .' He'd given her a little cuddle in the broom cupboard underneath his topless-lady picture.

They'd taken her out for a tipple at The Star in the evening . . . and then that had been that. She was finished. No more work. Thirty years over and done with in a blink.

From wherever she was in her house, she could see that square glass fang rising up. Whatever was she going to do with herself now?

Sue, her daughter, had tried to suggest things. Mam, why don't you go to afternoon bingo? Or you could go and help out at the hospital with the goodies trolley.

But she didn't want to be pushed around. She'd been responsible for her own life and theirs all these years. Her floors had shone; the desks had been lined up in neat rows; waste-bins emptied and shiny; lavs spotless . . .

What was she going to do? How she missed Marge and George and Billy! They belonged to a different world. She had to stop herself getting up at five-thirty to hurry off to college. At six she'd be looking at the wall-clock and imagining them all in their blue uniforms working the mops over the corridors. Billy and George would be slamming doors and seeing to waste-bins. Eight o'clock, snap-time. They were sitting round sipping milky tea and yawning.

Ivy felt deeply unhappy and unsettled. Was this the end?

And then she had the dream. Before her was a rippling expanse of blue water. Little eddies and frills twitched upon it. There she was, climbing down the steps into it; she, who had been terrified of water all her life, ever since a big kid had pushed her in when they'd gone to Madeley Street Baths from school. The best of it was, she didn't feel any fear. It seemed quite natural. Off she struck. She was gliding through the water. It made her feel so happy she wanted to sing, and it was warm, beautifully warm. She was soaring like some seagull, skimming weightlessly.

When she woke up, she was smiling. It was seven-thirty as well and not five o'clock. Around her clung the feeling of gladness. Nothing like that had ever happened to her before – not even with Ron.

Sue appeared with the push-chair and little Donna mid-morning.

'Listen, Sue, I've had this dream.' And she described it for her. 'I'm going to get down to the baths and learn to swim. I want to do like I did in the dream.'

'Don't you think you're knocking on a bit for that, our Mam?'

'Maybe, but I'm going to try.'

If she hadn't told Sue that she was going to learn, she would have abandoned the idea, but she kept looking out of the window at that big glass block and she knew she must do something. She was falling apart, like it was.

The next day she went into a sports shop in search of a bathing-costume. The last time she'd possessed one, it had had moulded bits like halved tennis-balls in the front. She'd bought it in the early days of her marriage to wear at Brid. on the sands, and every now and then she'd find her bust under her armpits or practically hitting her chin, and Ron had said, Eh up, our lass, what's up with yer knockers? Which had put her off even more.

Now she touched the swimsuits on the rails with nervous hands, looking for the infrastructure. There was none. They were just a smooth second skin with a few straps at the back. The assistant hovered near by.

'Can I help?'

'Yes, love. I want one for me, you know.'

'I wouldn't have the legs too cut away, dear, if I were you. They're for the, you know, younger end.'

'Yes,' Ivy said, 'a thirty-six – that pink-and-white-stripe Speedo looks smart . . . Oh,' and then as an afterthought, 'do you sell them orange armbands?'

'For non-swimmers?'

'Yes, love.'

Me, she thought, me in a Speedo swimsuit . . . they didn't appear to be called 'bathing-costumes' any more!

She decided the great event would take place that afternoon. Alone in her bedroom she struggled into the striped Speedo number. Although gravity had conquered most of her, her stomach still bulged and that wasn't padding.

She was too excited to eat any dinner, and anyway she remembered dire warnings from childhood about not eating before going in the water or your heart would give out and you'd sink.

The swimming baths was a bus ride away. And then she saw it; one like she'd visited in childhood. Its green onion domes pierced the sky. She took a deep breath and went in. She had to keep reminding herself of the dream as she faltered in front of the glass doors.

Before her lay the pool, blue and twitching slightly, as in her dream, but it wasn't empty. Youths with navy-blue squiggles on their arms and chests were plunging in, and young women in goggles threshed up and down the length, avoiding little lads who nose-dived constantly. One or two small children wearing orange armbands huddled uncertainly at the shallow end.

In the cubicle she struggled out of her anorak, navy-blue Crimp. trousers and jumper. On no account would she be taking her glasses off.

What a fool she felt as she eased herself down the metal steps into the pool! Once there she thrust her arms into the orange bands. The warm water lapped about her waist. It seemed altogether unfamiliar, but she watched the bodies of young men and girls scything through the ripples and she remembered her dream. It looked so effortless, in the same way seagulls hang in air-currents; she used to see them from the college windows.

She waved her arms about a bit in the water and experimented, rowing them round as she had seen people doing when they were swimming. What would happen if she were to lie on the water? Would she sink?

Someone zoomed alongside her and came up for air, then set off again up the bath, rearing half out of the water, plunging back again like some weird bird or sea-monster. In seconds he was back.

'You learnin'?'

'Trying, love.'

'You should hold on to the side and I'll show you what to do with your legs.'

He took hold of her ankles and worked her legs so that she felt like a frog.

'Just lie on the water, kick out a bit! What you got your glasses on for?'

'I don't want to miss anything.'

She was all of a dither inside and thought maybe she should go home. All right, she couldn't do it; too old . . . just not right. She was coming to bits; past it.

Nevertheless, when the man galumphed off again up the pool Ivy tried one or two experimental lunges. As the water sprayed her face, she got a shock, but gradually the movement of the pool and the excitement of flapping forward a couple of inches became quite pleasurable.

That day, she stayed in the water about half an hour. I'll come again tomorrow, she told herself. I'll come every day. And she did.

'Mam, whatever's happened to you?' Sue asked. 'You're never in and you don't come round any more.'

'I'm too busy for now,' she said. 'Later on, love . . .'

One afternoon she forgot her armbands. I'll make do without, she thought, and she launched herself on the water. She hadn't sunk in the dream, had she? With frenzied kicking and dog-paddling she managed to stay afloat. It amazed and intrigued her.

In that way she covered a width. This is it, she registered, I've done it! But there was no gliding about it; it was painful, ungainly splashing.

The day she actually swam up to the deep end, she was convinced her heart would stop, it was pattering so fast, and she expected to sink glugging to the bottom like an empty bottle. She kept near the side and pulled horrible faces if any lad popped up near her.

'You're doing all right,' encouraged the man who'd first helped her.

'Yes,' she gulped, as she prepared for the vast distance back, wondering all the time whether she could ever make it.

Months went by as she battled on. Up and down, up and down. Ten, fifteen, twenty. Lads steered clear of her because she wasn't above kicking them if provoked. The water spumed and glittered. Her efforts were all geared to the strokes, and when she wasn't doing them she saw them in her head, and they were smooth and gliding and mesmerizing. She kept at it with the gritty determination that had got her out of bed at five-thirty all those years and made her floors gleam.

On the day that she'd been in the pool two hours and swum seventy lengths, she suddenly became aware that she wasn't forcing herself any more; she was part of the frilling and the rippling; she was going with it and not working against it, and it amazed her.

Arriving home for tea, she found Sue waiting for her.

'Mam, I was getting real worried.'

'Gerraway,' Ivy muttered absent-mindedly. She happened to glance out of the window and she saw there was scaffolding up the sides of the college.

'Mam, what are you grinning at?' Sue asked, astonished.

Daddy's Boy

I'M JUST HOOKING UP this polystyrene carton filled with greasy chips and curry sauce when I see him.

'Hiya, our kid,' he says.

'Oh, Dad, fancy seeing you.' I haven't set eyes on my dad in a long while, because I don't live at home any more. I have this flat where I've got my stereo and things. I moved there when the Parks Department set me on.

'I reckoned I'd maybe run into you in here like. Your mam said to me this morning, "I do wish our Bennie 'ud come an' see us." I ses, "Well, 'appen he will, it being your birthday" . . . You've not forgot, have you, kid?'

'No, course I haven't, Dad . . . I'll be round later on.'

'Dun't that stuff stink! You have to pick it all up then like, do you?'

'That's right . . . But it's nice when we're planting – did you see them forget-me-nots? And the ducks have got babies – little yellow balls of fluff they are . . .'

'You're a nut case! See you tonight then.'

He swaggers off. I watch the way his shoulders waggle. He's a medallion man is my dad and his hair is kinky gold. He has a gold sovereign ring on his middle finger and he generally wears one of these leather bomber jackets and he douses himself in Brut 33.

When I was a little kid he was still going to sea. Mam used to get a taxi straight down to the docks to meet the boat the minute she heard it was coming in. If she missed him, then he'd roll up in a taxi hours later. I'd be up in the bedroom and I'd be peeking through the nets – it was safest to keep out of the way. I used to wonder why he was rocking about and singing. Then there'd be a screaming match. Once my mam locked him out and he battered the door down. Mind you, he had to mend it later and he thought he'd broken his big toe from the kicking.

I used to pray that my mam would get to him first before he'd treated all his mates. If she did, then they'd cruise up together in a taxi and there'd be bundles of plassy bags bulging with new clothes and they'd send my sister out for take-aways; and the next day a new suite or a microwave 'ud appear.

The day he'd be going back to sea there'd be a terrific commotion and my mam would be irritable, and then it would all subside: a kind of quietness would come over us. She'd be off to the bingo and I could start dressing up in my sister's clothes again; I had this old wig of Mam's – once I even went out in it but my dad caught me that time and he burnt it. When he'd gone, though, I used to feel I could breathe.

I finish collecting take-away dishes, lolly sticks, ice cream tubs, tab ends and cig packets – there's even used condoms – and I push the cart down the Gardens. I love working here. In summer there's all these kids laid on the grass with their shirts off; they've got their eyes closed and you can study the patterns of curls growing like fur to the waist-band of their jeans, and the sly pink nipples hiding in the hair, and their thighs bulging in the 501s.

There's seven-foot-high bulrushes in the pools, and water lilies like wax, and the ducks boat there. And there's all these heavy, sweet smells and that gives me time to think of my life. Or maybe I just float in these currents of sensation – like the scents from the geraniums and the rose-beds, or the way a kid walks so complete, with a slicking back of his hand over his hair, and his throat so thick and beautiful. I see all these things and I'm kind of burning with excitement.

But for me the worst time is the spring. The birds start real early and their voices are excited, and I know I'm waiting for something, just like when I was waiting for Shaun. That was the spring. I'm remembering Shaun now – I think that's because I'll be revisiting old places that'll bring him back. He lived next door to my mam and dad, and then he went away, and when he returned he was someone new and this kind of electricity zig-zagged between us.

One night we went to the Ice Maiden. All the time I was looking at him. He's very tall and dark and his skin is tawny and he has a square forehead and a way of brushing his hand over his long hair. A grey shadow runs down his cheeks. He watched me and I watched him and I was mesmerized. We had a few drinks and on the way home we landed up in this field and there was a white moon and the grass stood still and everything vibrated with us. Shaun was my first lover. The day he said he was off to London to work, I thought I'd die.

Ah, well, don't let me dwell on it. I'm going to take this prezzie to my mam. It's a glittery brooch I bought half price in Debenhams' sale. She thinks she looks like a Royal with her barnacle brooches clamped to her shoulder.

I shan't enjoy this get-together. I always feel nervous when I'm there – I have to be two people. The me that I am in my flat has to disappear and I play this dumb kid who's not properly clued up about anything but can run errands and carry bags in an emergency.

Each time I think to myself: Shall I tell 'em . . . shall it be tonight? And then I can't. I just know their jaws'll drop and my dad'll go crazy.

When I was eight or nine, I was sitting in the back of my dad's Avenger and him and my Uncle Alan were chatting. Usually they didn't notice me, because they seemed to be busy with themselves. All of a sudden Alan said: Eh, Trev, i'n't your Bennie a proper Jess!

My dad didn't answer. It was just as if he hadn't heard or didn't want to know. I sensed he was mad. Uncle Alan went rattling on. Alan's the type who would – he wears these white suits. You can never look at his face properly, because he likes you to study his profile. It's a bit like watching a weather-vane.

Well, my dad's mood, or whatever it was, just passed, but

when we got home my dad started shouting at my mam: I want that kid's hair cut off . . . he's not a bloody pansy . . . look at them curls!

I didn't know what all the fuss was about . . . but since then a lot has happened . . . What they don't understand is, I am as I am, and it's how I've always been – how I want to be.

I'm going up our road now. There's a long row of 1930s houses and they've all got their bubble-glass windows and coach lamps stuck on the wall and their Everest double glazing. My mam and dad's stands out because of its ruched electric-pink curtains and the pink plastic dahlias in the urn. It's called 'Chez Nous'. Visitors have to take their shoes off at the door. My dad's very much into DIY since he finished with the sea. He's even put in this electric-pink suite with gold-plated taps and he's rigged up a drinks bar with lights over it and stools.

My heart's bounding as I come up. They've obviously had the painters in at Shaun's old house. I've never really loved anybody but Shaun.

'Happy birthday, Mam,' I say as she totters towards me on her stilettos.

'Oh, hello, love – I've nearly forgot what you look like . . . Come and give us a kiss!'

I know I'll have a greasy red Cupid's bow on my cheek now. She smells of her Avon products. My mam's the colour of a roast Buxted chicken and she's got ruby-red lips.

'Do you like my new outfit, our Bennie?'

It's a two-piece made of Tricel – pink to match the curtains. She looks like a jelly-baby.

'Our lass, I don't go for them trouser things – they're too flappy. I've told you so before – I said, "Don't buy any more of them trousers, they give you a big bum." What do you say, our Bennie?'

Dad wants to push me into the firing-line but I won't have any.

'Oh, I don't know,' I mumble.

'Come on, get sat down – tea's ready – I've got you something real special.'

It's a big frozen steak and kidney pie that she's snaffled from work. She's about to lump a quarter of the stuff on my plate and I say, 'Mam, you know I'm a vegetarian.'

'Oh, you're not still on with that, Bennie, are you? I thought as you'd have give that up. Here then, you can have the gravy and your spuds and veg.'

'No, thanks, Mam, just potatoes and sprouts, please.'

They eat frozen sprouts all the year round, and they have a sort of bitter after-taste and they're mushy.

'You look real peaky, our Bennie – I know it's because you won't eat no meat. You need meat to live. Meat and two veg, that's what . . . I get real worried about you living on your own with nobody to look after you. I tell you who was asking . . .'

'Who?'

'Shaun . . . you know, Shaun Littlewood. He was here yesterday – got wed, didn't he.'

I can't get my breath. One of the sprouts seems to have got stuck in my throat.

'She was real bonny, his girl like . . . Funny he didn't ask you to the wedding, our Bennie.'

My heart's banging and I'm sweating. I wish she'd leave it alone, but she won't. I've got a pain in my chest, but I'm not sure that it's not a pain in my mind.

'Aren't you friends any more then?'

'Sure.'

'Well then . . . he could have invited you . . . Very posh it were. We had a sit-down meal an' all . . . roast pork with crackling – they daren't put beef on with that there mad cow and . . .'

If she'd just give it a rest.

'I wish *you'd* bring a tart home, lad. They keep askin' me at work. "When's your Bennie going to get spliced then . . . what's his tart like?"'

I can't bear it. I want to say it out and then she'll stop.

'Haven't you got a girl then?'

'No, Mam.'

'Don't you want one? All them you was at school with have got bairns now.'

'Have they?' I say and my heart's racing and I want to be sick. Everything's pulling tighter and tighter.

'You could put an ad in the "Together" column in the paper . . . every night there's a load of folk advertising.'

'Mam, I don't want a girlfriend.'

'Doesn't want one! Doesn't want one! I'd like to see my grand-bairns before I go . . . At this rate I won't, will I?'

Surprisingly, my dad comes in then.

'Leave the lad alone, Joan – it's his life, after all.'

'What – you're sidin' with him, are you, Trev? Sidin' with him!'

'Oh, Mam, do we have to have a bust-up over nothing?'

'You call it nothing . . . my son tells me on my birthday that he dun't want a girlfriend. What's up with you, lad? When you was a little kid, you'd never look a lass in the face . . . never. What's wrong with you? Are you that scared? Aren't you a man?'

It's coming now and I can't stop it. I'm shaking. I don't remember anything as bad as this – but I know I've been waiting for years to say it.

'Mam, stop pushing me . . . just stop it.'

She's staring at me and her eyes are wide open and she's gasping.

'You don't seem to understand . . . I'm gay.'

There's only the prim voice on telly saying, 'If the drought continues, we could be in for trouble next year . . . resources are being depleted at an . . .'

My mam's face is brick-red and her lips are tucking. 'I can't believe it,' she drops out. 'I can't believe this is happening to me, and 'appen you've got AIDS as well – yes, AIDS . . . oh . . .'

I look across at my dad. He's gone white.

'Steady up now, Joan, nobody said owt about AIDS.'

She goes for him then. 'It's you,' she hisses, 'it's you who's to blame for this . . . you've made him what he is. I allus knew . . . you're bent, aren't you . . . you and Alan . . .'

I catch my dad's eye and his mouth is working. There's a split second when I'm remembering him and Uncle Alan a long time ago. Uncle Alan's lighting a cigarette and slipping it into my dad's mouth and I can smell the L'Homme that Alan uses . . . and then they're arguing . . . just like Mam and Dad do.

'What's all this about then, eh . . . who's making accusations? Who said? You know that's not true, our lass!'

He's coming on real smooth, the proper medallion man. Because he's so busy denying it, Mam forgets me for a while. She's going to believe him, but he knows now that I know.

'All right, Trev . . . but you tell him . . . you tell Bennie that I don't want to see him no more . . . he's not to come here again.'

She's crying and I feel sorry for her, but I'm relieved because I won't have to pretend any more – I'm free.

My dad pats her shoulder.

'Now, Joan . . .'

'Tell him, then!'

'Bennie, you'd best be off. You've upset your mam, and on her birthday.'

I get up from the table.

'Tarra then,' I say. He won't look at me, but I can't wait to be out in the street and walking away, and it's as though I'm shaking free of a great big sticky spider's web.

Goodness

As they were crossing the prison forecourt, the wind slammed in their faces and made their hair twirl and their scarves flap. A man in heavy navy-blue official clothing came out from a guard box and produced a key which was chained to his body, and unlocked a metal door. Then they were crossing another yard and mounting some steps.

Lesley West turned round at the top of the steps; she was panting and coughing. She saw the spikes of the electrified fence and the billows of barbed wire. A dog-handler in a navy-blue cape patrolled below with his alsatian. Gulls hung in the buffets of wind.

'That's a bad cough you've got, Les,' Bill, the group leader, said.

'Yes, I've had it a bit . . .' Lesley clutched at her guitar; her heart was bounding.

The chaplain's face beaked at her. He had met them inside the prison compound. 'Are you, er . . . are you giving the address, er, Lesley?'

'Yes, John, I am.'

'Hope it, er, goes well . . . I don't suppose there'll be any, er, difficulties.'

He was leading them up stone stairways and his surplice became the dark beating wings of a crow as they climbed ever higher.

Uniformed men appeared at intervals and unlocked other doors. Then, after the unlocking of the final door, they saw the tiers of cells rising up as in some Greek amphitheatre, and in the centre was a net. Lesley West noticed a half-eaten bread roll caught in the meshes and a pair of torn underpants. Why had the underpants been jettisoned? she wondered. Had there been a fight? There was a dank, sour smell. Her heart was banging again and she gulped for breath and coughed, but she kept on smiling. Daniel in the lions' den . . . yes, that was it. They went into the fiery furnace and were not consumed . . . After all, this was what she had come for; she must rescue these sinners, save them from damnation . . . 'Yea, though I pass through the valley of the shadow . . .'

A couple of men with white, staring faces peered out as they went round the landing. Lesley hitched up her guitar case and prepared for another climb up to the fours. Through the steps she glimpsed other steps, a white billiard-ball head, a line of cell doors.

The Reverend John Booth marched into the chapel. The rest of them, amateurs, evangelists, blundered after him. Lesley was sweating and thought she might choke.

'I don't want you all sitting at the front,' Reverend Booth said, 'and don't sit down until they've all come in.'

Why was he saying that? Lesley wondered, and she could feel the moisture pooling down her armpits.

Phil Dawson was threed up with Steve McDowd and Chalky Stokes.

'Will we go to the chapel?' Steve said. 'It were a right laugh last time!'

'Aye, why not . . . passes the time. After twenty-three hours penned up in here wi' yous, it's time for a breather . . . I wish yous 'ud wash your socks!'

'Who's callin' who?'

'Na, you two, give us a break! Let's get ready for a few laughs. Phil did an impersonation of the Reverend. 'Now, chaps, let's say a little prayer, shall we?'

Oh, to get away from the other two's endless rabbiting: McDowd and his birds; Stokesy's case and I-didn't-do-it. He couldn't care less whether or not McDowd had two-timed his common-law wife and had this young bit on the side and another waiting in the wings – or that Stokesy had been fitted up by the pigs.

It was all boring; that boring he could jam the teeth of the both of them down their throats. McDowd had his Country and Western whining out every minute. Stokesy had a habit of cracking his finger joints and picking his nose. In the night he snored and there'd be this droning like jets going over and then a stutter and a few slucks and it would all start up again.

The wing p.o. unlocked them. Phil was just in time to see the group of visitors heading off into the chapel. Last was a real fat Jezebel. Her thighs were like bolsters and she had this marigold-coloured hair in a pony tail. You never got any pretty girls visiting nicks. They always had to be no-hopers. He supposed if you'd nothing going for you, prisons could give you something to do. Such a girl expected to see mass murderers, terrorists, rapists, bank robbers swarming about. When anybody on the out heard you'd been in nick, the first thing they wanted to know was:

What were you in for? What did you do?

He'd always felt that he ought to make something up: Well, I murdered this bird, cut her body up in inch squares and cooked her in a cream sauce and had her for me dinner . . .

I just robbed Barclays Bank of three million – a little job with a shooter . . .

His real answer was never more than a mumble to cover his embarrassment. He hadn't done anything spectacular – in fact his last crime had been the last of several undistinguished little light-fingered episodes; one of which had been the nicking of a consignment of teddy bears by mistake. But that had been the story of his life: the breaking and entering, all very skilfully carried out, to discover a cash-box with Petty Cash printed on the side, and crammed with loose change – copper and the new microscopic 5ps. It was a real pity that he hadn't been more successful. What he was good at, though, was gymnastics.

They all clattered along the paved landing to the chapel. The Remands were squawking at each other: there were some real young kids there – only about fifteen – and they were trying to rush across to the right-hand side, to which the cons were allocated.

As he sat waiting, he had time to take in the bird. She was standing at the front, blowing her nose from time to time and then strumming on her guitar. He studied her big, strong, fleshy face. Her eyes looked bruised, and she'd got cold sores on her upper lip. She wasn't looking at anyone, just twanging away on the guitar and singing to herself, real low. Her welting thighs looked real gigantic because of her Rupert Bear trousers and a chunky sweater bagging over the top of them.

A right lot of nutters always came to chapel.

'Hello, mate!' this kid rumbled. He was wearing wire-framed specs with no glass in. He'd been Phil's pad-mate one time, nearly sent him dotty because he couldn't shut up.

'How do?'

'Well, I've come here because I know . . .'

Phil shut off. His neighbour spluttered on. One or two blokes were sitting with their heads in their hands. The Remands went on twittering. The Reverend was glaring across from the side where he always sat when any group came in, so's he could take a skeg at what was going on, in case there happened to be a bit of violence. They were all going to have a laugh, that was for sure. The last time a party had come in from the out on a Sunday, this old biddy had pounded the piano, and a preacher and his wife bounced up and down on the front row to the music – even the cheeks of the woman's arse had quivered, and they'd all had these real stringy, churchy voices . . .

All the lads at the back had been snorting with laughter behind their hymnbooks at this lot yellin' and shaking, and the Reverend had looked furious. That had made it worse. Phil had guffawed afterwards until his eyes ran with tears.

At the end they'd come round pumping your hand up and down and saying 'God bless you' and staring into your face as though they'd gone dotty.

Phil waited, then this big Jezzy walked out into the middle at the front.

The preacher stood beside her and said, 'Lesley's going to sing for us first of all.'

She twanged a few chords on her guitar and then she started.

'Oh what a friend we have in Jesus.'

He was surprised at the sweetness of her voice; that such a fat lass with all those sores on her mouth could sing like that. For the moment his laughter stayed in his throat and he was content to follow the bright tones swooping in his head. She was beginning to puzzle him, the way this voice belonged to her great baggy body. He could imagine her in a year or two – she'd be one of them whose knockers hit their knees like bulging shopping-bags. Wait till she got into the God stuff, he'd be laughing then. The last time, when the other group had come in, he hadn't dared to look at Stokesy and McDowd.

'I want to tell you what happened to me . . .'

They were all staring at her now. Even the Remands had stopped giggling and shifting their chairs.

'All my life I've wanted to be good, and when I was sixteen I ran away from home and joined the Moonies. I stayed there for five years. I just wanted more than anything else on earth to be good . . . I was one of their best fund-raisers. I went all over London selling flowers. I raised thousands of pounds. But in the end I left them because I wanted to be good in a different way from what they said. Well, after that I got desperate. Believe me, I've tried all sorts – I've had every dope you could think of, and drink too . . .'

She was staring into their faces with her bruised eyes, and going on about wanting to be good but never feeling she was and then finally slashing her wrists.

'And there I was in this couple's house and I'd got blood on their £2,000 carpet – that was my second attempt to take my life – and I thought when I came out of hospital they'd not want to know me – I'd ruined their carpet . . .'

Phil missed a bit whilst he pondered on her wanting to be

good. It seemed a funny thing to want to be, good. Good for what? Good at what? Fancy someone being so bothered about it that they tried to kill themself! She must be getting near the crunch, he thought. He knew the pattern of these things.

'I felt worthless, do you understand? I felt nothing . . .'

There were tears in her big eyes and a lank strand of gingerish hair was falling down her cheeks.

Sure, he'd known moments of desperation – maybe when he first got nicked – but not to that extent, and then it hadn't been anything to do with being good or bad . . .

'And I rushed into this couple's bedroom in the middle of the night and I said, "Why have you stood by me?" and they said, "Because we love you." And then I asked them again and they said, "Because Jesus loves you."'

Phil breathed deeply with relief – at last she'd got there! He'd been waiting for it right from the start; in fact such a tension had built up that he was forgetting to breathe.

She didn't seem the same as when she'd come in. He found himself staring more than ever at her, wondering at her obsession with goodness. How had she started on it; was it because she'd not been able to get a lad? Goodness wasn't something he'd ever been excited about one way or the other . . .

What made the impact, though, was her getting so upset about it. It sort of spread on to people listening. Even the dummy with the glassless glasses had stopped rabbiting on while she was speaking.

They had a couple of prayers then and the preacher had his say and McDowd yawned and Stokesy picked his nose.

'Lesley will now sing "I Know that My Redeemer Liveth".'

Her voice took off, right up into the roof, and her eyes were real wide open and she was singing away over them all. And Phil saw her storming into this couple's bedroom – maybe the grey preacher and his dowdy wife with the floppy arse – and asking again and again until they said the bit about Jesus. Her eyes 'ud be smoking and she'd be lit up . . . Oh, her voice swept up again, and her eyes were shining. He didn't know what to make of it all – just wanted her to go on singing. It made him think of being a little lad and rushing into the sea at With. and floating on his back and gazing at the blue sky turning and feeling that he was moving with the clouds, and being happy.

They did a bit of praying – all the usual stuff – and then she came to the front again and said, 'If any of you feel you want to make a commitment to Jesus, would you like to speak to me afterwards – I shall be happy to help you.'

They all went banging out smartish, and Phil knew that none of them could cope with her because she was so big and ugly and would keep on about the goodness business like a lunatic. Until then he hadn't realized that it was all beginning to get to him. But suddenly he thought of her barging into that couple's room and trying them out and he felt dreadful. They'd all let her down again this time – they'd hared off, sooner than face her. It would have to be him. He braced himself for the moment of truth. It wasn't going to be something he'd enjoy, but he'd get through it somehow – anything was better than the thought of her thinking that nobody could be bothered with her. If good old Jesus could do it, so could he.

She was waiting at the door along with the landing screws.

'Oh,' he said, 'do you think I could have a word?'

'Sure,' she beamed, 'delighted.'

He tried not to look at her cold sores, which had a red runny crust on them, but kept his gaze dodging near her left ear.

'I've been thinking,' he said, 'how wicked I am . . . I done a very dreadful thing . . . cut me girlfriend up, didn't I . . .'

'Oh yes,' she said, as though he'd told her he'd caught a bad chill.

'And I need to . . .'

'Find Jesus . . . yes . . . ?'

He could see he had said the right thing. She was looking happier already.

'What's your name, please?'

'Phil, Phil Dawson,' he said.

'Well, Phil, we're having a discussion evening – I'll be coming in next Monday . . . then we'll talk about it. God bless you.'

She squeezed his hand. Well, he thought, he'd made the sacrifice basically because of her singing and because he'd never been able to bear feeling sorry for people.

With her voice still echoing round in his head, he made his way to his pad on the fours.

They were leaving now.

'You did very well, Lesley, are you all right? Want a throat lozenge?' Bill asked.

'Yes, please. Well, I feel quite pleased – there was this one poor chap who's approached me – he looked really haunted – I'm seeing him at the Forum on Monday – he says he feels he's a sinner . . . well, he did something really dreadful . . .' She shuddered and wouldn't say any more, but rising in her was a great leaping flame of elation . . . she, by her personal testimony, had saved, would save, a sinner. The man's pale face swam before her gaze again. He had blond hair and a neat, compact body. There was about his bumbling simplicity something truly beautiful.

When they were walking across the prison car park with the wind slamming their cheeks, she turned to the others and said, 'Do you know, I think my cold's actually getting better, believe it or not.'

As she drove back home, across the town to her small flat, she was singing again 'I Know That My Redeemer Liveth' and the notes soared higher and higher and mingled with the whirring and grinding of the engine.

Drowning by Numbers

I'M THE SORT OF KID who has crazes for things. Well, I reckon most kids do, but with me they generally last longer and they kind of take me over.

If I think back, I can maybe say the exact moment when this particular one started.

I'd just left school and I'd got a job in the S.S. office. It was boring – that boring you'd wish something, anything, would happen. Sometimes it did. Once this quiet woman – quite well dressed she was – started screaming. Another time this geezer pushes up to the counter and bellows, 'I've waited in here for two hours. If you don't see to me now, I'll wreck the joint!' This wanker pressed the button under the counter and the heavies rushed in and it was over in a second.

Well, even things like that get boring after a bit. You come to expect 'em and you can let your eye run over the room and decide which ones'll crack up.

Anyway, with me feeling fed up, when it got to dinner I went walking round in the town centre. Part of it was to escape the clueless type, Frank, who wanted me to have a sandwich with him. He liked to stand real close to you, munching cheese and onion crips, and they smelt foul in his mouth – and what with that and the crunching, it nearly drove me demented.

So I started drifting down High Street. I came upon this place jam-packed full of machines. I could see 'em through the smoky glass in the doors. It was dark in there and there were just these lights flashing – red, yellow, blue, orange. I've always liked being in these big, dark places like pubs and discos, where you can't see people's faces properly and there's the music going all the time. You'll catch sight of a bird's face and her red mouth and you'll think she's a stunner. If you see her outside you realize she's spotty and her make-up's that thick, if she came anywhere near you she'd leave a stain on your shirt like a burn mark.

Inside, everything's different. There's a kind of glamour. It's as though there's a promise; anything could happen.

That first time I stood watching this machine. There were pictures of apples, oranges, lemons, bananas. You slotted your 10p in and then it all came to life. A big chap with reddish-blond hair was feeding 10ps into the machine and there'd be a crashing and a whirring and sometimes 10ps came showering out. He stood there real cool like, and just shovelled this lot up with one hand and piled it on the top of the machine. I watched him put the 10ps back in. It got to the last one and this high-pitched tune jangled and all the lights flashed and pinged and another cascade erupted. This time it was quids and he just stuck 'em in his pocket.

I suppose what fascinated me was how cool he was but intent. His eyes bored into that console. He was balanced with one black baseball boot edged over on the toe of the other, kind of leaning into the machine.

All of a sudden, he turned to me.

'Do you want a go, kid?'

'Yes,' I said.

'Here, give us your cash!'

I handed him 50p in tens.

'Watch this and when it comes like that, use the nudge button!'

I followed his freckled hands poking the buttons. He'd be doing it fast but steady.

The first two tens nothing came up, and then bang, crash, wallop, it avalanched.

'Take it, kid!' he said.

I was nearly late for work and the light outside made my eyes sting. I'd got all these coins jingling in my pockets.

Somehow the afternoon didn't seem so bad after that. I was thinking how I'd go back there next day and I'd play on my own and maybe I'd win. And I wanted to be in that dark brown place with the lights glowing round the machines and the 'Space Invaders' warbling and whining. I wondered about the blond guy too: where he came from; what he did; how long he spent there; where he stayed; whether I'd see him again.

It started like that. I'd find I was processing papers all morning and I'd hardly notice that wanker Frank munching Tunes in my earhole and sneezing all over me and talking about what to do at dinner and whether he could get me a sandwich. I was concentrating on the machines and he was just background noise. I couldn't wait to be there.

Every dinner the man would be in playing the machines when I arrived. His square, freckled hands 'ud be feeding the slot and then there'd be the whirring and whining and sometimes a crash.

I'd begun to notice the regulars. There was this old bag with them winged insect glasses and blue hair. She plopped forty quid in – I know, because I counted – and she didn't get much back. When she'd done that, she'd pat her hair and leave, but somehow defiantly, as though she was saying, 'So there!'

This feller was called Shane, and when I started going regular to the Golden Touch he'd nod at me and say, 'Howdee,' and that 'ud be that. The second time I got a win after I'd put two quid in and my sandwich money, he looked across at me and nodded.

'Not bad, kiddo!'

He had this sly smile and his blond moustache lifted above his teeth, that were rough like him; rough but nice somehow. And him saying that made me feel like I did at school if Teacher ever praised us for summat . . . which didn't happen every day. 'Duane Appleby,' he'd say, 'you could go a long way if only you'd work . . .' But I wasn't interested; I'd be in the middle of one of my crazes and I'd have switched off to everything else.

Now these machines all have some sort of system: you have

to sus 'em out. It was Shane who showed me that. If the manager gets the idea that the punters are grabbing too much, then they withdraw the machine and a new 'un will be installed – a fresh challenge . . .

When I'd run out of the ready, I'd just stand there watching Shane play. I never saw him leave and he was always in there when I arrived, always the same. He wore a black bomber jacket and a check shirt, designer jeans and baseball boots.

After work at night I started dropping in to the Golden Touch on my way home. At that time there'd be a different crowd, but I'd find Shane still leaning by a machine, watching the lights and feeding coins in.

'Are you working late or summat?' my mam asked when I started this routine.

'No,' I said, 'me and this kid just dropped into the boozer for half a pint.'

'You don't want to start that – you'll get to be a proper alco like your dad.'

Dad was out at the local every night; that was just part of his way of life. My mam had the telly. It was never switched off. She said it made her nervous when there was no sound, so anything you ever said to her got all mixed up with 'Take a tablespoon of sugar' or some geezer getting his brains blown out somewhere.

I was her blue-eyed boy though, because both my dad and my brother, Clint, worked in a goodies factory, and I'd got an office job and wore a collar and tie and after-shave and looked smart.

After her little quizzing, I realized I'd have to find another excuse. If I said working late, she'd expect a cut of the proceeds.

'Have you got a girlfriend?' she asked.

'No,' I said, 'not on your bloody life.'

The day I was three-quarters of an hour late back from dinner, it was only Frank who saved me from getting done. This other kid had tried to sprag me to the under-manager. Of course after that I had to listen to Frank whingeing on about his mother and how she was a slag and how he hated her and how no birds fancied him (what do you expect with green teeth?). I pretended to be interested but I was listening to the clacking and thundering of the machines. I knew their box shapes; the designs on their consoles; the pattern of nudge and press buttons.

Lasses often played 'Desert War'. They'd be zapping Arabs for all they were worth, tilting over so that their faces were practically smack up against the machines.

I suppose all this was going on a long time. I didn't really notice much, because I was concentrating that hard. What I did notice, though, was that I was always short of cash. I'd given up eating at dinner but I had to find my keep at home or my mam would start noseying.

'Lend us a couple of quid till pay day,' I'd find myself asking Frank. He'd grumble a bit, but he paid up. I didn't worry too much, because I might win. The only snag was, if you came up, you had to stop yourself playing your winnings back in again. Shane and the old bag with the insect specs never took anything away, or so it seemed – the old bag no question. With her, it seemed she couldn't leave until she'd got rid of her loot. There were a lot of old biddies like her; they'd come crabbing in with their shopping-bags when they'd drawn their pensions.

I knew why they came, though, it was this feeling of, well, it might happen . . . it might be next time. When the quids came pelting out down the metal shoot, it was as though you'd struck buried treasure. That was something I used to dream of as a kid; somewhere I'd come upon a hoard of fabulous jewels and I wouldn't have to give 'em up to some dead-beat museum. I think there was maybe something else as well . . . but I'm not sure about that. Anyway, there was a thrill to it. You were in it, against those square, jangling boxes – they were robots with chiming voices inside and they mesmerized you. They locked you into their rhythms but you were struggling against 'em as well. It would be either them or you. All the time I'd be in the gloom with the boxes tinkling and whizzing, I'd have my stomach screwed up with excitement. It might be the big one; it just might be. You'd have dreams of faraway places – these white beaches and boats rocking on lemonade sea like you see in Bacardi ads. There's always these birds with cut-away swimsuits that leave their bums sticking out at the sides like cushions.

It was the day I'd had a warning from the boss about time-keeping that the first thing happened. By this time I hadn't paid my board for a month and my mam was getting snappy; plus I owed Frank quite a bit and I'd fallen behind with the payments on my compact-disc player.

Anyway, I couldn't get down to the Golden Touch quick enough after work. In there I could forget everything else. I was feeding my last couple of quid into this machine and taking it very steady. You see, when you've heard your final 10p go click and there's no music and no whirring, you get to feeling kind of empty and desperate and you want to cry or scream or kick the bastard. I wasn't aiming on reaching that point too quick. I figured if I went slow and spun it out, I'd have more fun.

Well, I put in about 50p when I saw this bird had come up to Shane and was standing by his machine. I'd never seen anyone accost him like this before. They all knew him of course and you could tell they liked him, but nobody interrupted his playing.

'You promised,' she said, 'you did promise.'

She was tall like him and had a fantastic body. She was wearing these black leggings, and you couldn't miss anything, and about five-inch stilettos, and her hair was fastened up on top of her head in a blob. If she walked down a street, I bet you'd have guys crashing their cars to stare at her.

He was looking into her face and smiling, the way he did, with his moustache lifting, but he was still playing.

'No,' I heard him say, 'I've not forgot.'

Then there was something I couldn't follow and she turned right away. She had to pass near me to go out and I saw in the lights from the machine that her face was shining with tears.

I thought maybe Shane 'ud stop playing then and follow her, but he didn't, and when I left because I'd spent all my sheckles, he was still crashing the knobs and had his eyes glued to the console.

I was serving a week's notice when it happened. The fact that the boss had finally fired me didn't really bother me on one level . . . I couldn't feel it. It was just words. My mam and dad took a different view.

'I suppose you'll be stuck about at home now, under everyone's feet. I can't think what you've been getting up to – what's wrong with you, Duane?'

Oh, I maybe smiled at her and put my arm round her waist and tried to be the usual cocky old me. It was only by doing that that I'd managed to keep her from throwing a wobbler about the keep money I hadn't fetched her. Like I say, she still had this memory of me as the blue-eyed boy, but it was wearing a bit thin.

It was a real relief to be in the Golden Touch. I'd been there maybe ten minutes when I heard this godalmighty smashing sound. At first I thought something had blown up, and then I saw Shane. He'd got a big claw-hammer in his hand and he was laying into the machines. He'd smashed up the front of one already. Bits of glass and rivers of coins were leaking out and it was vibrating and twittering in a kind of indecent and spooky way because he'd just killed it.

Next thing an alarm went off and a load of cops pelted into the room. All the grannies were shrieking and cowering in a corner. A posse of blue uniforms were trying to get hold of Shane. It was just as though he'd flipped his lid. I thought of that girl in the slinky black leggings: her big red mouth and her wide stride; the way her breasts pouted and her face was shiny with tears.

I was standing near the door as they led him away in handcuffs, and I got to see his face close to. He was like a man in a dream and his eyes were staring right through me, through everything.

Maybe it was the cheese and onion crisps I'd scoffed on my way there, but whatever it was I suddenly had to rush into the lavs and throw up.

Since then, with me being on the dole, I'm watching telly and videos a lot, but when I go to sign on I find I'm always looking for her. I just can't get her out of my mind: her big dark eyes, her red mouth and the tears . . .

Self-Improvement

It was a combination of three things that made Betty Spinks do it: Sid, her husband, had just covered up his bald patch and whistled off to darts for the fifth evening running; Nial had gelled his hair and rushed out in a little T-shirt to a disco and it was a freezing night; she'd had a row with Clark over that slag he'd had in his bedroom.

Bloody men, she thought, nowt but trouble. I'm sick to the back teeth of 'em all . . .

Then she realized it was the start of the German Conversation class. Her friend Val, at work, had pushed her into enrolling – but once she'd signed the form, she'd known that she wouldn't be going. She always found it very difficult to say no. That was how she'd ended up married to Sid. He'd badgered her until she'd given in. This thing with the night classes had been the same too: Val had been on at her to go:

Oh, come on, Bet, everybody's learnin' languages now. There's going to be all these foreigners comin' here – maybe we'll go there . . . to work, you know . . . You know, European whatsit . . .

European hospital cleaners, Betty had sniffed, but she'd gone with Val and enrolled. And this was the first night . . . She'd intended to forget; just tell Val some cock-and-bull story if she rang up:

Our Nial's badly again with his chest . . . can't leave him, love . . .

But somehow now, standing in the living room looking at the big scene of snowy peaks and lakes and mountain chalets that was done in wallpaper, she thought: Bugger 'em, bugger 'em all, I'm off!

She puffed upstairs and put on the frilly white blouse and Courtelle two-piece that she'd had for her daughter Tracey's wedding and she stood in front of the dressing-table mirror covering up her broken veins with pancake and powdering here and there. She even experimented with the brushes Tracey had given her at Christmas and splattered on some blusher – not too much though because she might come all over scarlet with one of her hot flushes. The bride's mother, she registered, peering at herself.

The phone rang. It was Val.

'I'll meet you at the bus stop, Bet.'

'All right, love.'

As the bus rumbled and droned into town, Betty began to feel bilious.

'I nearly didn't make it,' she told Val.

'Oh, how's that, love?' Val was just lighting up one of her endless fags. When pressed at work she'd even dob the ash in her overall pocket.

'You know, work an' everything . . . Our Nial . . . I've told our Clark that if I catch him upstairs with another tart I'll be telling his dad . . . and he won't like that . . . well, I mean to say . . .'

Really she wasn't thinking about them at all, she was dwelling on the ordeal ahead. She'd never been any good at school, couldn't seem to follow. When Miss Phillips was holding up the flash cards with the numbers on, she'd panic and there was nothing in her head at all, just water.

You've nothing between your ears, Betty Logan, Miss Phillips had said.

It had been a relief when her mam had kept her off to look after the younger ones . . . The best had been Domestic Science, but even that had been scary – like when they'd been making pastry and hers had been too wet and her mate had said:

Shove more flour in quick, Bet . . . and she'd plopped in a white mountain and stirred like mad, so that by the time Miss West reached their table, it looked like white plasticine.

The college was massive and there were all these green plants in troughs.

'Bet they take some dustin',' Betty said.

'Very like.'

'An' if they get broke someone'll be for it.'

In the marble-floored foyer stood lots of notice-boards bearing all manner of messages, and young women tinkled to and fro in smart little suits and blouses and the air was sneezy with expensive scents. Young chaps in designer jeans chatted in groups and there were clutches of important-looking manager-type men wearing suits.

After some frenzied consulting of the notice-boards they dared to ask one of the Christmas tree ladies.

'First floor, room 122,' she treacled, looking past them.

'Aye, it would be,' Betty muttered.

'Better get in t'lift, Bet . . . come on.'

'I don't trust them things – might get stuck.'

They heaved upstairs and Betty thought she could smell her underarm deodorant. She wished she'd given herself an extra spray, just to make sure.

'I don't know as I'll get the hang of this lot,' Betty mumbled, 'don't know at all.'

Already about thirty people were sitting at tables which had been set in a circle.

'I shouldn't 'ave come,' Betty said, 'I don't know about any of this.'

'It'll be all right – good for a laugh.'

'Some laugh!'

The Miss came in then. She was a young woman with sleek short hair and glasses, very smartly dressed.

'Guten Abend,' she said.

Val giggled. Everybody grinned and some said 'Guten Abend' back.

'Know-it-alls,' Betty murmured to Val.

'Oh, there's allus some.'

The Miss kept pointing at herself and saying, 'Mein Name ist Samantha Jones.'

'Oh, that's her name then . . .'

There was a deep silence. Samantha Jones told them her name again. Betty was praying that nobody would ask her anything.

'I'll die if anybody asks me,' she whispered to Val.

One by one people said their names and the Miss nodded and smiled and passed on to the next person.

Betty sat, her armpits wet with terror, watching Miss Phillips holding up the sum cards between the tips of her white fingers . . .

You've nothing between your ears, Betty Logan.

'Wie heissen Sie?' The question hit her like a piece of chalk, straight between the eyes.

'Say your name,' Val hissed.

'Betty Log . . . er, Spinks.' Betty felt a hot flush zooming up her neck and tingling in her cheeks. She wanted to escape, but she couldn't. The question had passed on. She was steaming hot.

A man with grey wavy hair who was sitting opposite her gave her an understanding smile and she managed to grimace back. At least he looked sympathetic – well, she'd noticed him struggling himself and trying to laugh it off.

Teacher was writing on the board. It was white and shiny and she used a blue marker pen. There was no more chalk and clouds of dust and Teacher blowing on her fingers and coughing. It was all very smooth.

At half-time they were allowed to go into the corridor and Val had a fag and joked with a couple of young punk girls and a chap who sold German cars. The grey-haired man kept glancing at Betty but she pretended to be reading her book.

At nine o'clock, when it was time to go home, Betty said to Val, 'I don't know about this German lark, Val, don't know if I can manage it again – all them funny words and them two dots and that *der*, *die* and *das* business.'

'Oh, go on.' Val started laughing and broke out into her deep smoker's cough. 'You should 'ave seen your face when she said "Wie heissen whatsit"!'

'It weren't funny . . . If I look sharp, I'll be back before them lot get in – they'll not know as I've been out.'

And indeed Betty had the kettle boiling and the ham sandwiches and biscuits on the tray by the time Sid lurched in.

'We never won . . . bloody rotten game,' he growled.

Betty didn't listen, she was trying to remember how you asked a person's name in German. Wee something – what was that *Sie* thing?

'I'm talking to you,' Sid yelled.

'Oh, was you, love, sorry.'

'What's up with you then?'

'Up? Nothing, love.'

But there was.

The next day after work Betty shot off into town on her bike.

Well, I'll just go and look at it, she thought – I don't need to buy it . . . I'll just have a look.

The German books were on display in the Foreign Languages section. Betty took one down and flipped through it. There were pictures of spotless towns, historic places with quaint inn signs; beaches with giant basket things on them in which people evidently sat.

She turned the book over and looked at the price: £7.95. Eight quid, a lot of money – eight quid. She hesitated with a hot flush pending and then she scooped the book up quickly and went to the pay desk, her cheeks flaming. What right had *she* to be buying a *German* book!

The journey home was arduous as Betty was cycling into a headwind, but when she reached the estate she found herself peering about her at the high-rise flats and the bleak square blocks of gardenless houses – Giroland it was called. The open-plan lawns were pocked with fag packets, drinks cans and dog turds and the wind slammed by them. She seemed to be seeing them for the first time.

They were marooned out there, a twenty-minute bus ride from the city centre, with their own supermarket, clinic and three pubs.

She planned how she would have a good look at the book anyway – well, she'd have to keep going to the classes now that she'd bought it.

When she reached home, she hid the book upstairs in her sewing things so that none of them would know. She could just imagine Sid's response:

What – Sprechen Sie Deutsch! Bloody Krauts, what do you want to learn that fer? We beat the buggers, didn't we!

By the second week they'd progressed from 'My name is' to 'I live in —, where do you live?'

They had to break up into groups and ask one another questions. On no account must they speak English.

After two more weeks Betty knew that the nice grey-haired man opposite in the blue zip-up had a son and daughter, a Ford Sierra car, a TV, a video, a washing-machine, a dish-washer.

'Dish-washer' was a lovely word – *Geschirrspülmachine*. Only a young married couple apart from Ken said they had one. Val nearly lost her top dentures trying to say she hadn't, and then she collapsed in a coughing and giggling bout.

The following week Val was badly and Betty wondered if she dared go on her own, but she did. When they broke up into groups, she found herself partnered with Ken.

'Mein Name ist Betty Spinks,' she laboured, staring at her notebook. He was grinning at her.

'Wo wohnen Sie?'

'Oo, what's one 'er them?'

'Live,' he said, 'you know . . .'

'Oh yer – ich wohne in Hull.'

The man turned the pages of his notebook. Betty thought he looked desperate.

'Ask me if I've got a telly,' she prompted.

'Oh yes . . .'

She told him she had a six-bedroomed house (a lie), a TV, a video (a lie), a washing-machine (it was always breaking down but she couldn't tell him that), a dog (a lie); and she didn't mention Sid, or Nial or Clark.

Ken's Ford Sierra was red and his hobbies were DIY (what a useful man!) and cooking (better still). He hadn't yet mentioned a Mrs Ken.

Betty searched in her book to find out how she could say 'Have you a wife?' What she was really enjoying about these classes was the way you began to know all sorts of things about people: the kid three up from her on the left for instance was twenty-two, had a blue VW, lived in a flat and liked drinking and squash.

Hah, there it was, *haben*, 'to have'.

'Haben Sie . . . Frau . . . ?'

'Frau? Woman? Nein,' he said, and gave her a deep trusting smile.

On the bus on the way home Betty let herself dream about Ken, who must now be bombing homeward in his red Sierra. She had half hoped that he might suggest giving her a lift, but then of course she couldn't have accepted one because she didn't want him knowing that she lived in the estate. He of course lived in one of them new detached houses with pillars before the doors and bubble glass in the windows and coach lamps. She'd always fancied something like that.

When he arrived home, he'd start cooking Schnitzel and Pommes frites in his fitted kitchen and he'd be drinking Rheinwein. They'd learnt about ordering food – Kuchen mit Schlagsahne, cakes and whipped cream. It all sounded much better than cakes and cream.

She'd only just got her coat off on arriving home when Sid plonked himself down in front of the telly to watch snooker.

'What's for supper, our lass?' he grunted without turning round, as though he'd never been out.

'Oh, a sandwich,' she managed. She'd nearly said 'Kuchen mit Schlagsahne'.

The week the class watched the video of Bremerhafen and Duhnen, Ken sat beside Betty. He'd said to her 'Guten Abend, Frau Schmidt,' because Miss often got her to read Frau Schmidt and him to read Herr Schröder. She'd gabbled 'Guten Abend, Herr Schröder.'

'Eh,' Val said, 'I think that Ken fancies you.'

'Oh . . . gerraway!' Betty said, trying to sound innocent. She'd put on a new Lurex jumper that evening and violet eye-shadow.

'Yer, I'm sure he does. He always asks you questions. Why did you tell him you was a *Verkäuferin*?'

'Well, I allus fancied working in a shop selling stuff – anyway, it sounds better than *Putzfrau*.'

Betty was feeling quite carried away by this wonderful world of clean streets and spotless houses and tourists riding in traps across gleaming stretches of dunes to an island. No muck, no take-away dishes stuffed in bushes and empty drinks cans and fag packets . . . And beside her was Ken of the red Sierra. It 'ud be quite something to be perched in one of them carts at the side of him, off to see the wonders . . .

Even when Nial rang the door bell to be let in at three a.m., sloshed out of his mind, and later peed the bed, and she discovered Clark bedded down with a lass and snoring, Betty didn't let it get her down. She felt like some fairy princess and she couldn't wait for Monday evening.

During the week she studied her book and practised to herself until she could carry out a regular interrogation and could have given directions to the station, the cathedral (unfortunately there wasn't one), the toilets, the museum, the town hall and the stadium (there wasn't really one of those either).

One Saturday afternoon when she was biking back from town after a shopping spree in which she'd bought herself a German dictionary, she was just passing the Arctic Ranger, a pub not far away from their street, when she saw Ken getting out of a Robin Reliant which was parked in front. From the passenger side a pruny-looking woman with grey permed hair emerged.

At first Betty had wanted to call out, but then she knew she mustn't. For sure that was Mrs Ken – it had to be.

Sid was watching *Saturday Sport*.

'Bloody beat,' he said, 'out of the league.'

'Oh dear,' Betty murmured, 'I'd best get the kettle on.'

As she waited for the kettle to click off, she changed the Reliant into the red Sierra and made Mrs K. into his sister . . . Guten Tag, Herr Schröder.

Promotion Prospects

IT ALL HAPPENED because on this Monday morning I didn't feel too good. The night before, me and Debbie had had a Chinese – she'd had sweet and sour pork. Mine was sweet and sour prawns.

My mam was out cleaning and my dad had left home at seven-thirty to be at work for eight. I rang up Mr Barnes, the manager.

'I'm sick, Mr Barnes, got some kind of stomach bug,' I said.

'All right, Andy, stay near the toilet. See you termorrer.'

'Thank you, Mr Barnes.'

Barnsy was grooming me up to be under-manager and I had to keep on the right side of him. I pictured him strutting about in his pin-striped suit. You could always smell him before he appeared because of his after-shave. If he wanted a particular girl on the check-out, he'd ask her to work late on Thursdays and Fridays and maybe give her a lift home in his Escort. He liked me because I was smart. I'd had a regular Saturday job in the supermarket since I was at school. A couple of mates had as well. Me, Kenny and Mel used to be having a great time mucking about – we were supposed to be filling up shelves and unloading boxes from delivery vans. We only dared do this when we knew Barnsy had cleared off somewhere.

Just popping out to head office, he'd say, and then we'd wink at each other.

One Saturday afternoon he must have arrived back early unbeknown to us, and that was when Kenny and Mel were having a wrestling bout in the back. They were panting and squeezing each other and I was egging them on from the sidelines – and it was kind of exciting and hysterical. Kenny had a very compact build, did weight training and used to play in the first soccer team at school.

Ger him, Kenny . . . come on . . . get a lock on . . .

I don't think Barnsy saw me, because I was on the far side behind a pile of crates.

All of a sudden I heard this voice:

You two lads – you're fired. Don't think I'm paying you to ponce about in here . . .

I banged straight back into the shop. He never knew I'd been there, and after that I was very careful.

When we left school in the summer he took me on permanent. He thought I was steady – well, I always did what I was told; plus my mam's always insisted on me being smart – short hair, clean shoes, collar and tie.

Inside I'd kind of wanted to be different – I'd wanted to push things a bit . . . know what was on the other side . . . Kids like Kenny and Mel, for instance, they'd be getting up to all sorts – never really spelled it out, but you felt they were living. They were at the weight training every minute and down at this health studio place and moving about in the city pubs.

You don't want to be hanging round with roughnecks like them, my mam always said. Anyway that Kenny's mam's real dirty.

My mam had had this thing about cleanliness as long as I could remember. She got my dad to help her decorate every year. She was never satisfied with how things were. You could eat off of our toilet floor. There were these pale-blue fluffy mats and blue fluffy toilet cover and even the toilet-rolls had to be put in this blue fluffy tube with a bow on top.

She cleaned for quite a few folk. There was this lady who lived in a big mucky house and taught somewhere. She'd been giving my mam stuff for years. My mam came home with these trophies – once it was big boxes of PG tea-bags with tea-pickers on the side to make you feel they were real healthy. Anyway, this lady was throwing 'em out because she said there was aluminium in the bags and it 'ud send you bonkers. Mam said maybe we were mental anyway already so it didn't make much difference and she took 'em.

I was dressed in the cast-offs from this lady's kids all the time I was at school – that was when my dad was redundant. Her kids went to Oxford University – my mam knew every time they even farted.

It was not that my mam finished with the cleaning. No, there was more to it than that. She wanted to be improving all the time. We'd had to have a new roof with them modern tiles, Everest double glazing on all the windows and front door; a microwave; fitted kitchen and bathroom.

My dad was tall and thin and he had a bad chest. He'd sooner let things be, but my mam wouldn't, and it caused a lot of rows. She'd start stripping paper off and then go down with one of her headaches.

I can't stand it . . . can't do no more, Joe . . . I'll have to leave it to you.

If he was badly as well, then there'd be trouble. It was as though she wanted to force him by being ill, and if she couldn't, then she'd kill herself, just to show him.

I was thinking about this after I'd rung Barnsy, because I was sitting in the toilet staring at the door. It was still covered in pink undercoat. My dad was supposed to be glossing it but he said the fumes from the paint made his chest bad. Of course, him being a painter and decorator, he was breathing it in all day long. My mam's attitude was always: Why should other folk get their places nice and us not?

There was another thing too. She and her mate Barbara were always talking about other women's houses:

Oh, she keeps a dirty place . . . never washes her nets. Look at her winders! People like that . . . and her kiddies . . . it's not right, is it?

They thought if you weren't washing and cleaning you were rubbish. You'd committed a crime and it was about on a par with murder.

I knew my mam wouldn't mind as long as I looked smart;

nothing else really mattered. Because I was wearing this suit and not a red overall the colour of the crossing beacons, she was satisfied. She didn't want me in a boiler suit and workman's gear, no, not at any price.

This queasy feeling wouldn't stop. I didn't know what to do with myself. I put my stereo on and listened to a couple of tracks but I didn't feel right at all, so I just sat in my room and moped.

I'd never been allowed to do as I liked in my room, because my mam 'ud be bottoming it every week and she'd chuck out anything that I'd be working on. Models made mess; books trapped dust and took up cleaning time. She didn't mind stereo and compact-disc players. I had my chest expanders under the bed. She'd allow that. Once I'd got these porno mags from this kid at school. I'd forgot and put 'em under the bed. She found 'em and raised the roof.

I won't have you lookin' at that sort of thing. It's a disgrace . . . To think a son of mine . . .

Her face went all red and puffy. She wouldn't touch 'em even, but stood over me while I burnt 'em in the back garden. The pages fluttered open and I saw her staring at them, though she pretended she wasn't looking. When my dad came in from work, she said, Joe, that lad's had some dirty books.

Where are they? he said.

I've made him burn 'em – discustin' they were . . .

That's right, he said.

Well, you tell him, Joe . . . you tell him!

Half the time my dad couldn't be bothered, he just wanted to get out into his shed and hammer a bit.

What with the tune on the stereo and feeling kind of low, I started thinking about Debbie. Now, I'd been at school with Deb. She was what you'd call a nice girl: little and blonde with one of them raggedy perms, that she gelled. She'd wear these little white blouses, 501s, white socks and Doc Marten's and have a gold cross and chain round her neck. My mam liked her, knew her mam and dad.

When we'd been going out six months Debbie said one night:

And, what about you and me getting eterned like?

So I had to buy her this eternity ring, which meant I was real strapped for cash for ages.

At school, kids used to look at us and say, The Lovers – suppose you'll be getting wed soon?

When we've saved up, Debbie always said.

She went into a hairdressing apprenticeship as soon as she left school.

I want me own shop, she kept on saying. I know just how I want it – beige and cream . . . deep shag-pile carpet . . .

We'd spend any of our spare time going round the shops when they were closed, just looking in the windows. That was our night out.

I want a leather three-piece suite. And, and a big colour telly and a video. I'd like our front room to be all white: white carpets, white suite . . .

I'd to hurry up and get to be manager so's they'd provide me with a car. She was hankering after a Sierra. My dad had a Reliant called 'Kitty'.

It occurred to me, sitting there, that Deb was rather like my mam. Deb wanted to be making things better all the time too, only unlike my mam she concentrated on people. When we'd been touring the shops the night before, she'd kept on looking at other girls and saying:

She looks real cheap, a proper slag. She ought to have her hair cut properly – she's too old for that long hair. That's dead common. Look at her . . . discustin'!

She'd be re-dressing 'em – shoes, skirts – the lot.

A long while ago she'd started working on me. I'd had to buy a leather bomber jacket and save up for these thirty-pound shirts. She chose my after-shave, my shoes, my socks. One Christmas she bought me a gold-plated identity bracelet.

When we were coming back from the take-away last night, who did we run into but Kenny. He just looked at me. He was in this white T-shirt and Levi's. He walked with a swagger and he'd got his hair in a flat-top – and there was me in me bomber jacket and all me fancy gear.

Hi, he said, how're things? And it all came out real lazy and I could feel his eyes flickering over me.

I was dead embarrassed but I wanted to talk.

We can't stop, Deb said, just got our Chinese and it's going cold . . .

It hadn't registered with me at the time, but now a sort of restlessness knotted up in me. I wanted to get out.

By this time I'd been mooching around that long, it had got to dinner. I didn't feel hungry but I had a sudden idea. If I could sweat it all out of me, I was sure I'd be better. I wanted all this rotten, yucky feeling to go.

Now I started thinking about Kenny and Mel again. They went to these sauna baths, they'd said how it freshened you up and was a laugh. Right, I thought, I'll get off there. Me mam wouldn't know – anyway, what was wrong with the bloody sauna?

Somehow, once I'd fetched my bike from the shed, I began to feel better. Perhaps it was sitting inside that had been making it worse.

It was down a side street in this big old building. I could see the sign over the door: Sauna and Health Studio. At this time they'd be arguing about who was on early dinner and who had to have late. Old Barnsy 'ud sometimes be missing for a couple of hours. Long lunch, he called it. Long lunch!

The lasses thought maybe he'd have a bird stashed away somewhere. Suddenly I was real glad that I wasn't at work.

I paid my money and this feller in a navy-blue tracksuit told me to get changed in one of these cubicles. You were to strip off and then sit around in this steam place with your towel round you. If it was too much for you, you'd to have a shower and you could go and lie in a cubicle on a bed for a bit afterwards, if you needed to.

Some were having massage, I think, because I passed this room and I could see a great big bird pummelling this bloke who was lying on a couch thing. Her face vibrated as she slapped him about. She was more like an all-in wrestler than a bird. I thought I wouldn't have liked to be on the wrong side of her.

Next to this massage place were the cubicles. It was a narrow corridor, all tiled, and I happened to be looking for one to change in, when I saw this bloke lying bollock-naked on a lounger in a room. He had big dark eyes and he was smiling. I went all hot and confused and I shoved on to the end, where I found an empty cubicle.

At first when I entered the sauna, I couldn't see anything properly because it was all crammed with grey fog. The heat made me blister with sweat. Then I'd make out some faces. Fellers were just sitting there on the benches, sizing you up. What struck me was I must have been the youngest there. They were mostly old blokes, old enough to have been my dad – but there were some in their thirties, I should think, as well. And they were all staring, looking as though they wanted something . . . it was like hunger on their faces. In this mist it made me feel real weird. I kept remembering the bloke on the lounger. He'd called out to me. What would have happened if I'd gone?

You couldn't see anybody too clear and I didn't like to look. It was creepy, the way you'd see a piece of leg and a foot or a chest . . . and sometimes a towel had kind of slipped . . . There was this feeling that anything might happen. I was excited in a funny sort of way. It was like nothing I'd ever known.

Water was running down my armpits and my face was all wet.

I started to feel a bit panicky and I thought I'd best get showered.

I'd turned into my cubicle when someone came in after me. I knew it, because I could feel him behind me, and for a fraction of a second I thought it might be the man I'd seen earlier, and I was transfixed . . .

'Now then, who's a big boy then? This what you do when you're sick, is it! You and me'll have to make a date . . .'

It was Barnsy. Without his specs and with nowt on but his towel round his waist, I hardly recognized him.

'You're a well-set-up lad, Andy . . .' he said and he was right close up to me and he'd whipped off my towel. I felt sick.

All the time I thought: This isn't happening to me. I couldn't seem to do anything. I was mesmerized . . . it was as though it had to happen to me and I couldn't avoid it. Barnsy's shoulders were pink with heat and I saw some moles on 'em. I seemed to be looking down on what was going on, at these great wedges of pink, hairy flesh. It reminded me of sides of pork at the butcher's. There was this green curtain over the door, and I thought: Green curtain . . . green . . . and I remembered them tea-pickers on the tea-bag box.

'Come on,' he said, 'bend over, I'll not hurt you . . .' and he pushed me against the wall. And it hurt shocking but I couldn't say anything and my heart was bumping and bumping and then he went out and I was on my own.

Must get out of here, I thought. Where can I wash? Must wash . . . must get Barnsy's stink off me . . . must get back to me mam's . . . must scrub it off . . . must have a bath.

I climbed on my bike and started pedalling home and I found that I was shaking, and I still had this feeling that it hadn't happened to me.

After an hour I came out of the bath and I changed all my clothes and made myself a coffee.

While I was drinking the coffee, I started seeing the bloke on the lounger who'd had that sad, longing sort of smile, and it made my heart hammer. Then I was wrestling with Kenny that summer before we left school and he was forcing my head down . . . the smell of his sweat . . . little things you don't forget . . . the way his thighs bulged and his shoulders were really quite narrow but the muscle bulked them out . . . the cleft in his chin; the very definite V of his lips.

Thinking about the sauna bloke and Kenny made me drive out Barnsy, but then the picture came back again: Barnsy pink and warty pushing his awful old man's cock at me, and I thought I'd vomit.

When Deb phoned later on to see if I wanted to watch telly at her house, I said I wasn't feeling too good.

'I'm just resting up, like,' I said.

'Oh, go on, And . . . shall I come round there then?'

'No, Deb,' I said, 'not tonight, love . . . like I say, I'm feeling a bit off-colour.'

By the time I'd put the phone down, I'd made a decision: I wouldn't go out with Deb any more. I'd have to ring her up and tell her – but for now I just wanted to think about what had happened . . . or rather what hadn't happened . . . and all the time I kept on seeing this guy's eyes staring at me, and then it got mixed up with Kenny's shoulders and Barnsy's awful cock.

Restitution

SHARON TOOK HER FACE very seriously. She stood now before her mirror, preparing for the disco, and studied it. Would tonight be the sweetie image with the wedges of wire-spring curls surrounding the milky chocolate oval; or would it be the face of a Yoruba mask with a bare, high, polished forehead and the hair drawn up into a tight topknot? There was another face too – a lush, whorish one, of heavy eyelids and pouty mouth – but that wasn't one she tried to assume, it was more how other people saw her.

Tonight would be hair up, she decided. She tried her profile; stepped back and forth; pirouetted.

From downstairs came the faint vibration of *Neighbours*. Mam and Brian were watching telly. It was almost like old times, but not quite.

Her return was chivvying her with unease. She hadn't known that going away to college would make her so aware, so critical of everything at home. Mam was jumpy and very much concerned with convention. She centred on boring, ordinary things; was a woman with short, blow-waved hair who wore jumpers and skirts which were shrouded in pink and blue check nylon overalls when she was at home. Her feet were encased in fizzy pink splodges because Brian bought her a new pair of fluffy slippers every birthday, as though he couldn't think of anything else. Brian was nice but he didn't have much imagination, except when he was lying under cars with a spanner in is hand.

It's lovely to have you back home, love. I've had a vacuum through your room – we've been decorating – well, you'll see, we've done the hall – I wanted that little pink flower paper again, but Brian wasn't too keen . . .

Yes, she'd said, yes, Mam, and grinned at her and Brian.

Everywhere seemed poky in the terrace and a lot of the talk ran on double glazing or fitted kitchens or new bathroom suites. Mam and Brian paid regular weekend visits to Texas, the massive DIY emporium. Sharon hated it with its bile-green rubber plants, and pink and blue and mushroom ceramic tiles, and baths and bidets with gold-plated taps. The latest was conservatories, but how you could have a glass box stuck on to the back of your terrace, Sharon couldn't imagine.

She took off her granny glasses and, whilst she was urging her left eyelid open and floating the tiny wafer of her contact-lens on to her eyeball, she thought how her mother was one big contradiction.

To look at Mam, you wouldn't imagine that she had been swept off her feet by a Nigerian student (Sharon's father) and had once lived in Lagos.

I met him at a dance in the City Hall . . . I was seventeen. I'd never had a boyfriend . . . seventeen! We danced all night. He said he was a prince . . . and he was wearing this navy-blue pin-striped suit. When we drove up home in a taxi, my mam nearly had a fit.

Sharon knew fragments of the story, gleaned by careful questions over the years. Once she'd come upon a black and white photograph blobbed with damp, which her mother kept at the bottom of her scarf drawer. A big man, black as coal, stood stiffly, arms linked with a thin-faced, smiling girl. The photograph made her mother's paleness contrast more sharply with her father's darkness. She'd studied that picture, hoping to find some clue.

But what was it like out there?

Oh, there were these white villas with terrazzo floors – but we didn't live in one of them – we were in a tin-roofed shack in a place called Surulere – there were open drains and flies swarming over 'em and the kiddies played among the muck all day long. His family were in and out every minute – you couldn't keep anything in the fridge . . .

To think she'd been born out there, born in the shack at Surulere; but she couldn't remember a single moment of it. Mam had left with her when she was eighteen months old.

He'd got this other family see . . . there was this woman and three kids and I never understood . . . You hadn't to ask, not anything. He'd go out and that 'ud be that . . .

I never thought I'd see home again . . . it wasn't home there . . . not with all them flies and the heat all the time. And the food . . . I couldn't eat their food – that foo foo was like big balls of white plasticine.

But, Mam, Sharon had asked, when she was little, why ever did you marry him?

Her mother couldn't say . . . but Sharon, as she flicked on mascara and smudged wings of beigy gold over her eyelids, followed her mother's voice back over the years and was still searching for a clue.

He said he was a prince . . . oh, such a good dancer . . . in this pinstriped suit, and he smelt of scent. His white shirt was starched that stiff it cracked and the knot of his tie shot straight out from his throat and his ties were beautiful – always dark and silky, and there was a matching handkerchief. He powdered his cheeks. A prince, my mam, your nana, said, what, a prince!

Sharon's grandfather had been a trawler cook and had gone to sea at fourteen . . . all the men had been to sea.

Oh yer . . . every couple of weeks there'd be this little death-notice in the papers:

LOST AT SEA

He had muttered about Can't stand bloody darkies . . . you'll not marry a darkie. But she had.

All through Sharon's primary and junior-school years, she had been conscious of her brownness, her difference from the rest. The lads had called, Nignog, blackie, blackie . . .

There was the day the big lad, Craig Lawson, and his mates

had shut her in the broom cupboard. She'd heard them chanting 'Blackie, blackie . . . go home, blackie' outside. But she hadn't cried – she wouldn't let them see. Finally the caretaker had found her and had released her.

She'd run all the way home at three-thirty to avoid having to listen to their taunts or have sticks hurled at her. Her mam had been in the living room when Sharon had rushed to the mirror over the sideboard and had stared at her face.

Mam, Mam, I'm not black, am I? Mam, I'm like you, aren't I . . . I'm white like you?

And her mam had said: Course you're not black, Shar, you're like me.

In a fit of rage and despair, because Sharon had known it wasn't true and that her mother wouldn't face it, she had picked up a brass elephant and hurled it at the mirror, which had smashed.

Shar, you naughty girl, whatever did you do that for . . . seven years' bad luck . . . whatever for?

Just when she was putting the finishing touches to her geranium-red lips, the chimes went on the front door. It would be Tina, her old school friend. She had only reached the head of the stairs before Brian was welcoming Tina in:

'Hello, love, how are you then?'

'Oh, fine, thanks . . .' Tina was standing grinning up the stairs.

'Hi,' Sharon called, 'come on up.'

They lurched to and fro in Sharon's little room, laughing and full of pleasure at being together again.

'Seems ages!'

'Yer.' Sharon spun round on one black plimsoll. 'Does this look okay?' She was all in black – black clingy top, black leggings – apart from a minuscule scarlet and black frilly skirt. In her ears dangled a huge silver crescent moon with a star caught in it, and on her wrists two dozen thin silver bangles slithered and clinked. The red of her skirt was taken up by her big pouty geranium lips.

'Fantastic! Hey, do you like College then, Sharon?'

'It's great . . . I love being on the stage – it's what I want to do – there's that feeling – it's that scary it makes you want to throw up, and then you go on and it's like the most wonderful thing that ever happened.'

In the last week of term, she'd got up on the stage at the college disco and sung 'Lipstick on your Collar' – she'd not known she would dare. The vibrations of it lingered around her and the faces of her friends gleamed with pleasure. She was on that high again. It came when she was dancing too; rocking into the beat, feeling it throbbing up from the floor until it took her with it and made her part of it.

'How's work, Teen?'

'I'm bored out of my mind – nothing ever happens in that office.'

Soon they rang for a taxi and sat close together on the back seat, laughing about nothing at all.

'Does it feel good to be back, Shar?'

'Oh God, Teen, I don't know . . . part of me feels kind of split in half.' She couldn't really say to Tina: I'm not sure where I belong . . . well, I sort of am . . . but I don't think it's here with my mam – it's with my friends, or out on a stage.

'How do you mean?'

'Well, I never liked it here much . . . if you know what I mean . . . and now I'm somebody else.'

The gleaming Christmas streets flashed by – red, gold, and blue lights on artificial trees, and shiny black pavements. Sharon thought of her mother and father riding home in that taxi after the dance . . . She'd met her father once. He'd come to England when she was fourteen.

Shar, I've had a letter, your dad's coming over – says he wants to see you . . .

She'd been caught in curiosity and anger. She'd had years of being called nigger and blackie and hearing gags from lads about her thick lips and her pan-scrubber hair and her NHS specs. She had been locked in this ugliness and she'd looked at the pictures of girls with long gold hair – Rapunzels letting down their braids for the prince – and she'd burned with longing and hopelessness. Her mother had been offhand about the meeting.

If you don't want to, you needn't . . . I mean to say . . . never shown any interest before . . . why now?

But she'd met him. He had taken them to a pizza place for a meal. He'd been a burly black man in a suit who mopped his face with a very white handkerchief and wore several big rings on his fingers and gesticulated a lot, flashing his yellow palms. The whites of his eyes were brownish. She had not been able to think of him as Mam's husband, or as the man in the taxi – the one who would be her father.

Hello, little girl, he'd said, hello, little girl.

She hadn't been a little girl. At fourteen she'd already been shooting up – not yet her eventual six foot, but still very tall for her age, and beanstalky; a girl with a pimply forehead and long thin legs. He'd seemed disappointed, she'd thought, because she didn't know what to say and had played with the doughy pizza. They never ate out in a restaurant, couldn't afford it. He was a businessman, so her mother 'ud said, and could afford it – though he'd never ever sent them any money.

After that there had been silence – a total silence; he had sunk out of sight. She didn't think of him, had no need to learn anything more about him . . . but now on this evening, coming back to the city where she had lived for nearly all her twenty years, the old wound seemed to have opened . . .

Inside this beautiful person that she had become, vestiges of the past lingered. She was also the ugly, bobble-headed kid peering earnestly through her glasses that were stuck together at the bridge with pink Elastoplast.

The evening spun before them.

'I'm that glad you're back, Shar . . . I've really missed you . . . had no laughs since you went. It should be good tonight. I've hardly been since you left.'

'Yer, I'm looking forward to it.'

Sharon smiled, remembering past Saturday nights dancing until her legs ached and her plimsolls were worn through and her clothes were steaming; and swopping stories of boys, and clothes and music and grouses about home . . . me mam said and . . .

They stepped into Spiders like two princesses. Fifties and sixties tunes shook the walls. Lights flipped on faces and on pint glasses standing in glistening rings on tables.

'Like a drink?' a kid said, popping up. It was somebody she knew from her 'Goth' days – black leather trousers, black sweater, shaggy black hair, and shades, an array of silver sleepers, crosses and skulls hooked in his ears. She'd loved the drama of the Goths; all the black, and the deep maroon and purple lips, the black nails, spiked up black and purple hair. Now she was creating her own image, which still had hints of Goth blackness. She liked to tour tat shops and hunt through racks of second-hand clothes for something eye-catching – for ages she'd had this men's dinner jacket, bought from the Cancer Research shop, made of black wool gabardine, beautifully cut and with sweeping satin-faced lapels. She'd wear that over her white broderie anglaise blouse and her black leggings, and when she walked out like that, men swerved their cars to peer and whistles resounded and she stalked on with her shoulders back, taking no notice.

They settled themselves at a table and the lad came back with two half-pints of cider for them and they grinned and said cheers and he flopped down opposite them.

Before them figures gyrated in the honey-coloured gloom and the DJ's voice yelled and coaxed and announced and a fresh burst of rhythm made the floor dither.

'Come on, come on . . . let's . . .'

And they were up all together, shaking and writhing with the beat, and it was a sheer thrill for Sharon, and now and then she would catch Tina's eye as she slithered her feet and let her hands and arms shimmy in the swell of sound and her waist shook too, all of her was eeling in the rush and eddy.

Now and then she'd see eyes watching and she'd gaze beyond them or through them – meet the concentration and throw it back. She could do that now because she was powerful. She was the black, elastic performer who could cast a spell. This casting of spells had come to her gradually; she didn't know from where . . . only that whilst she was doing it she was supremely alert, tense, and yet relaxed. It was like loving in its starkness and strength.

The record came to an end and they flocked back to the tables. Cigarette smoke drifted in swathes; the light caught beer in glasses and moist red lips.

'Hi,' someone said, 'hi, I've been watching you.'

He was a big kid in a white shirt and his hair was brushed straight back from his face in a thick wave. He had the handsome, ruthless face of a male model – the type who pose in expensive suits and shirts for glossy adverts.

The moment Sharon looked at him, she knew. Tina didn't, because Tina hadn't been at her primary and junior school – she'd only met Tina at the girls' senior high. This person belonged to the days of the broom cupboard. She was sure it was Craig Lawson. But he hadn't recognized her and wouldn't. He had no idea of her transformation at sixteen from the shrinking brown kid into the beautiful black woman.

Tina was staring and gave her knee a nudge under the table to indicate her enthusiasm. What a boy . . . what a fantastic, yummy boy!

Sharon felt quite cold.

'Have you?' she said, and she let her gaze spin in front of her over the waves of dancing people.

'Yes,' he said, 'I couldn't stop looking at you.'

'Oh.' She smiled and drew a pattern in some cigarette ash with a spent match.

'Dance?'

'All right.'

They were moving together. Chubby Checker, 'Let's Twist Again'. He was twisting down, zigzagging his smart leather casuals and then rising up again, holding her all the time with his eyes. She swung her hips and wiggled her pelvis and sang the words.

'Come on,' he said, 'next one . . . Where have you been all my life?' He was laughing and she looked at the fine pale column of his throat. His jaw was square and slightly cleft – a very regular, handsome face – but she looked at him and through him to something else.

Maybe half an hour they danced, maybe more, and he never once lost her with his eyes and she danced out of herself, mesmerizing him. She was giving herself to the moment, to the music – and the music belonged to another generation and that lent her a disguise.

A smooch came on and he held her against him, fitting his smart casuals about her thin black plimsolls. His hand was on her waist, the fingers splayed. He was holding her with a sort of care. It was not a grab or clutch, because she looked too exotic for that and she was giving nothing away.

'I've never been here before, is that why I haven't seen you?'

'I'm just a visitor,' she said, gazing over his left shoulder.

'You can't be.'

'Oh, but I am.'

'Well,' the DJ crooned, 'let's have one of the Master's now . . . the unbeatable Elvis!'

Some people clapped and the thick throbbing voice came on. 'Teddy Bear'. People jived and swayed and shook, all breaking loose and moving back and forth, as the voice sang.

'I love Elvis,' Sharon said, 'and Marilyn Monroe – beautiful, doomed people.'

He didn't answer, he was continuing to look at her. She pretended she wasn't aware of his concentration.

'I think I'll have a drink now,' Sharon said and broke away from him at the end of the song.

Tina was waiting for her at the table. 'You're doing well there,' she whispered.

Sharon sat back and picked up her glass and sipped her cider. 'Oh, I don't think it's anything like that.'

'You must be joking – he can't take his eyes off you.'

'Things aren't what they seem, Teen.'

'What do you mean?'

'Never mind.'

He was back. His pale hair was like a flame and he had this winning way of staring into her eyes and smiling, but she couldn't forget the broom cupboard. Things don't change, she thought, not inside . . . and she wanted to confront him with it, make him own up to what he had done, make him pay. That long humiliation didn't just disappear in an evening . . . No, they were only wearing disguises.

When he told her his name, she said, 'Yes, I know who you are.'

'But you couldn't,' he said, still smiling.

'Oh yes . . . we were both at Bricknell Primary. You were ahead of me though.'

'I can't believe this.'

'In fact,' she said, feeling how her heart began to bang, 'you once shut me in a broom cupboard.'

'No,' he said, 'that's not possible.'

'Oh yes,' she smiled, 'that's how it was.'

They were dancing again.

'But I've never seen you until now.'

She gestured it all away and turned into the music, losing herself in it, whilst he studied her.

And then came the last number and they were all up, swilling to and fro with the hot voice of the synthesizers. Sharon felt the passion pressing her, forcing her, but she wouldn't succumb. The ball of rage at the centre of her was still there . . . it was the injustice, the cruelty; the shit she had had her face forced into. It poisoned you: you suspected people's glances, casual remarks, things half heard. Everywhere you sensed derision and you knew that you didn't belong. When she saw black people in the street, they would stare at her, and in their looking she would see a certain acknowledgement, a recognition, and they would pass by. They would claim her if she wanted . . . but did she want?

Now they were all embracing. 'Happy Christmas!' and they were kissing each other.

'Happy Christmas, Shar!' Tina said and threw her arms round Sharon.

'Thanks, Teen, and you . . .'

He was holding back, standing beside her.

'Happy Christmas,' he said.

'Thanks,' she smiled.

They were all pushing out now, some staggering with the booze, and they stood in the street waiting for taxis. Cars sped by into the shining darkness. It was a place of factories and docklands and breakers' yards, and women didn't walk down there alone at night.

Just then, as they lingered, Sharon and Tina and Craig Lawson, trying to break away, a flash black car swerved up. Sharon thought it might be a taxi, but a couple of men in leather bomber jackets sprang out – bruiser types with big coarse faces.

'Now then, sweetie, what about it?'

One of them had come right up to Sharon and he seized her arm and began to drag her away.

'Get off me,' she snapped.

Everything juddered and rattled. She saw Craig Lawson go for her assailants and punch the first guy, but he was then whammed across the face and seized by the second fellow, forced on to his knees and knocked to the ground and booted by both of them.

'Stop it, stop it!' Sharon heard herself yelling.

Somebody was phoning for the police. The club bouncers raced out and joined in the fight. It seemed to be going on for ever. She was a bystander, listening to the bumping and blundering of her heart.

They heard the moaning of a police siren. Blue lights flashed; the two bruisers shook free, slammed into their car and took off into the night.

Craig Lawson was lying on the ground with blood oozing from his nose and mouth.

As Sharon knelt beside him, waiting for the ambulance to come, she found that she was crying. Tina, standing close by, kept repeating, 'I never thought this 'ud happen.'

Sharon put her hand on him then. 'Thank you for what you did . . . They'll be here soon,' she said, and she looked away down the dark blue oily road.

Somewhere out on the estuary a ship mooed. She knew suddenly that her mother must have gone with her father all those years ago, and almost been destroyed by him, because of her yearning for the unknown and the exotic . . . She had thought she'd live in a marble-floored villa and have white peacocks strutting in the garden. She would escape the back-to-backs and find a new world. In the end she had settled for Brian, the motor mechanic, a house smack bang in the middle of a terrace. And she, Sharon, was left, the creation of a dream . . . and maybe that was a rather miraculous thing . . .

The ambulance men were very kind and matter-of-fact. As they were carrying Craig away on the stretcher, they turned to her.

'Will you be going with him, love?' they asked.

'Yes,' she said, 'I will.'

Destiny Waltz

WHEN LES HAD SCARPERED with Max, a young waiter from the hotel where he was chef, Annie's Yorkshire puddings had taken a nose-dive.

She'd stared at the flat brown splodges on the baking-trays and had been reminded of her first sponge cake. Instead of standing in a golden peak when she had edged it out of the oven, it had whooshed down in the middle and gone splat. She had glared at it and, in a rage, had hurled it into the nearest bin. Never again had her sponges sunk. She had been cooking all her working life, fettling away for most of it in the kitchens of the Rose and Crown.

On the day the Yorkshire puddings had collapsed, she'd stood at the steel sinks and thought: It's time you packed it in, Annie, lass – you've had enough – aye, you've bloody had enough: forty-three years turned into Black Forest gateaux, wedding cakes, french fries and steak, burger and chips, scampi and chips, steak and kidney pie . . .

I'm goin', she'd told Alice, her assistant.

Gerraway!

Oh yer, I've done my whack . . . I want to live . . .

Alice couldn't believe it. She'd stared at her as though she'd lost her marbles.

You'll maybe think different termorrer . . .

No . . . I s'll not . . .

The kids, Darren and Kerrie, were married and lived away, so she didn't have to think about them. She was on her tod. When she opened the door of her semi, that was it.

On her last day at the Rose and Crown, they'd had a knees-up and presented her with a Binns token.

We thought as you could get what you wanted, Alice had said.

That's very nice of you, love, I'm real choked.

Well, after that it had all gone quiet. She didn't know many folks round about, what with her always having been at work. And all the work lot were still at it. When you'd retired, what did you do? She'd had her head filled with joints and sauces and orderings and timings for years and years. Twelve was twelve, it wasn't one-thirty, and seven was seven and not eight. It had been like one long examination. If the punters complained, you were for it. The kiddies had once had a hamster, and the way it footed round on its treadmill had reminded her of her own life.

And of course Les had worked what they call 'unsocial' hours, so she'd find herself slapping the chip-pan on at any time, day or night, when she happened to be in. Naturally he'd never cooked at home – not on your nelly. Cooking was what he did at work with his chef's hat on and his whites. She, doing the same job, had just been the 'cook'. Annie, everybody had yelled, Annie, what shall we do?

After a fortnight at home, she'd felt unhinged. She couldn't be doing with meals for one, and she'd vacuumed throughout every day, polished the windows, had the china cabinet out, and had stared at the Binns token propped up on the mantelpiece in the front room and wondered.

Here she was, still with some go in her, just stranded. Les used to say she had a good leg on her . . . Mind you, in view of what had happened she was beginning to re-examine everything he had ever said about her.

She had been used to rattling about hither and thither, and all that energy sizzling round inside her made her dither with nervousness. Radio 1 was going full blast, and she hummed along and trilled now and then and waltzed a bit until she banged into the suite or the drinks trolley (Les had been a big one for drinks trolleys and ice buckets – not that they'd ever used them – just for dusting over, she'd muttered; or breaking your leg on.)

With Radio 1 still booming in her head, she'd decided to pop into town, and she was just pedalling down the road when her eye happened on the notice-board:

TEA DANCES, *every Wednesday 2–4 pm* 50p

It was propped up outside the swimming baths.

That's it, she thought, tea dance . . . tea dance!

She saw herself gliding across a glassy ballroom floor or whizzing in a spin-turn. She was sixteen and dancing at the City Hall on a Saturday night and watching the rainbow bubbles spilling over people's faces as the big crystal ball in the ceiling caught the light. The women's scent and the smell of Brylcremed hair had made her heart patter. Everything had been shining and the singer up at the microphone had oozed and crooned. 'Destiny Waltz'. And during 'Destiny Waltz' she had met Les, her destiny.

In a dream Annie dismounted and wheeled her bike up to the doors of the swimming baths.

'Er . . . can you tell us about the tea dance today?' she asked the receptionist.

'Oh yer, love, same as usual. Afterwards a lot of 'em have a go in the pool – you could bring your cossie . . .'

'Thank you,' Annie beamed and then she soared off on her bike to spend the token in town.

She bought a big black sports bag and a white towelling leisure suit and a slippery blouse that looked like leopard skin.

It felt a bit peculiar, going off to dance at two in an afternoon, but she stood in front of her wardrobe mirror, fluffing out her scrambled-egg hair and fixing in her gold hoop gypsy earrings, and studied herself. A good leg . . . got a good leg on you, you have . . .

She wiggled her right leg about a bit and decided she didn't look too bad. She sprayed herself well behind the ears with some scent Kerrie had brought back from Benidorm.

It was as bad as being sixteen and getting ready for the City Hall. They'd all be down in the basement cloakrooms fighting and elbowing to get a place in front of the mirror.

You had to reapply your lipstick and powder – even though you'd only just done it at home twenty minutes before – it was just like icing a wedding cake, piping on all the rosettes and twirly bits.

As she cycled to the baths, she floated to and fro over stretches of gleaming parquet. The band was brassing up, the vocalist was caressing the microphone and her heart was skipping.

She was going to meet her destiny again.

Soon she had paid her 50p and was mounting the stairs, sports bag in hand. Afterwards there would be the pool and later she would change into her towelling number.

In a drab, moderately sized room, groups of grey-haired bulgy ladies were gossiping at tables. All the furniture was of the tubular metal variety and the legs, Annie saw, were of a dingy red. On a long table covered with a white paper cloth stood a tea urn and piles of cups and saucers. At the far end a young chap was messing about with a hi-fi system which kept letting out hiccups and gurgles and sudden wails.

One or two men were engaged in conversation in another corner of the room. It had been just like that at school: girls at one side, boys at another – even in the playground.

The ladies were giving her the once-over, she noticed. She made her way towards a table.

'An' I said to our Jean, it dun't do to let 'em stay out till that time, and she said, Mam, you don't know – when you was young it were different . . . and I said . . .'

They all seemed to be gossiping about the grand-bairns or bingo or some private scandal.

'I wonder if he'll come, then,' one woman was saying. She had very pink cheeks and a sprinkling of warts near her chin. 'You bet your life that Eunice'll be straight after him if he does. Bold as brass she is, that one. She's got such a neck on her.'

Annie bought a cup of tea and inspected the rim of the cup to see if it had been washed properly. She felt her mood going splat and she had a sudden memory of the Yorkshire puddings. They'd be coming to the end of the lunches by this time and would be wrestling with the washing up and thinking about a cuppa prior to the next influx at dinner-time.

The young chap stepped up to the microphone and, after some deep gurglings, he jollied them along:

'Ladies and gentlemen, here we are for another swinging tea dance . . . Take your partners for the first waltz.'

A booming and crackling followed and then the music began to warble, though always with muzzy undertones of distortion. This wasn't exactly the band brassing up at the City Hall and the vocalist's voice swooning in the flood of sound.

Annie looked about her at the knitted ladies dipping biscuits in their tea and patting their hair.

'And do you know, she had it all took away,' her neighbour was confiding to her friend, a lady in a boring Tricel dress.

'You don't say!'

'Oh yes, she had to.'

Annie began to feel a wave of panic surging up her chest. It was all about nasty operations and diseases.

'One day she was as right as rain – I saw her at bingo – and the next she found as she'd . . .'

A couple were taking to the floor. Their sloping bellies nudged each other as they moved. Annie thought of wide skirts flaring about glossy thighs, and long black side-burns like pieces of felt, and shiny black wavy hair.

'And now, ladies and gentlemen . . . get ready for a . . . wait for it . . . a foxtrot.'

The beat was quick and zingy. Several couples got up and performed, but it was all very sober and careful.

Annie sat there in her leopard-skin blouse and tried to concentrate on her cooling tea.

There were, she noted, a lot more women than men, and judging from the fragments of conversation she kept overhearing they were mostly widows.

Just then a man came over.

'Care to dance?'

'Oh yes,' Annie beamed. She was up in a trice.

'Haven't seen you at these before.'

'No,' Annie murmured, 'no . . . been at work.'

'I see. I come reg'lar . . . since the wife was took . . . When she went, I didn't know what to do with meself.'

'No.'

Annie was so busy concentrating on avoiding his shuffling feet and being rammed by his belly, which kept swinging at her, that she was incapable of talking.

He was just leading her back to her table, when through the door strode this electrifying figure clad in a sharp navy-blue blazer and grey flannels, and a blue and white spotted tie, and with a matching hanky lolling in his top pocket. His grey hair was slicked back and he had big bold brown eyes and a Roman nose. Everything about him proclaimed his dangerousness.

A wave ran through the tables of grey permed ladies. Annie saw how they were peeking up.

'Hello, Geoff,' one of the men called. The newcomer nodded in the man's direction but kept on towards Annie's table.

Annie knew he was making for her. A tango was just starting. Oh, she thought, it was just like being sixteen all over again, only a hell of a lot had happened in between: steak and kidney pies; shepherd's pies; jam sponges; treacle sponges; wedding cakes; jam tarts; and Les, and now Max, the waiter. She felt she'd never got to grips with Les. At least with the cooking she'd mostly been able to . . .

'Now then, perhaps you'd like to tango with me?'

He had a rather nasal voice, much softer than she had expected. She'd thought it would be clever and harsh.

Oh, he was a very smooth dancer. In no time she was swaying back and letting her head tilt at an angle, whilst he fixed her with those bold brown eyes. There was a faint pinkness in his cheeks, and his fingers were soft and white. She was gliding under the crystal ball again and glimpsing their reflection in long mirrors. His narrow, shiny shoes positioned themselves exactly by her black patent court shoes. His hand played low down on her back, directing her.

At the tables gossip hopped in the teacups. She could just imagine what they were saying:

'Look at her, dressed up like a dog's dinner . . . what a neck . . .'

But then, just when they were tangoing like mad, Annie saw the apparition dizzying through the swing-doors. Another movement rippled the permed heads.

This mauve-haired piece teetered into the room. Her cheeks glowed with tropical tan and she had a scarlet Cupid's bow mouth. She wiggled in her black ski pants and big purple mohair sweater covered in little pearls and shiny bits.

The dance finished. Annie watched how no sooner had Geoff led her back to her table than he was making a beeline for the brazen piece who had just come in.

Annie's neighbour said, 'Eh up, just look at that Eunice – see 'er. I said as she would, didn't I! Just look! Oo, she's a man-eater is that one . . . her husband died of a heart attack.'

It sounded to Annie as though the woman thought the mauve-haired siren had killed her husband.

'Yer, as soon as that Geoff comes in she's after him. They say as she's been married quite a few times – any man . . . yer not safe with such as her.'

'Oh.' Annie concentrated on her empty teacup. She would have liked another dance. Her eyes followed the mauve-haired Eunice and Casanova Geoff. Everybody was staring at them.

'Well, ladies and gentlemen, that's it for this week, I'm afraid – so here's your DJ signing off.'

There was a gulp and a click and the cups and saucers rattled and everybody began to get up and leave.

Annie followed the group down the stairs and turned left into the labyrinthine women's changing rooms.

By the time she was sliding into the pool, the others were already standing in groups in the water, their bathing-hats pulled well down, their heads nodding, still gossiping. Then she saw Geoff porpoising up the bath. He reached the deep end, flipped underwater and was soon heading back. When he came up beside her, she gave him a big beamer.

'That's clever,' she said, admiring his seal's head.

'Oh, is it?' His soft, weak voice amazed her again. 'Are you swimming up then?'

'Might as well.'

In one movement he had passed her. She continued with her laborious breast-stroke. When she reached the deep end, he was waiting for her.

'I can't do the crawl,' she said as she hung on to the side. 'Nothing fancy . . . never could.'

'Oh, I'll show you – come down to the shallow part.'

He demonstrated, placed her arms in the right position. 'Which is your breathing side?' he asked.

'Right, I suppose.'

She set off, struggled, flapped her arms and sank.

'Don't let him start teaching you,' a harsh woman's voice said.

It was the mauve man-eater, Eunice, and she was grinning. Her mauve hair had disappeared under an elaborate cone of rubber flowers.

Annie resented this intrusion. She felt Geoff could have gone on demonstrating until she drowned – she didn't care, she just wanted him to continue.

'He always has to show the new ones,' mauve Eunice went on. 'Men allus like showing you things, don't they!' and she actually winked. Annie was taken aback.

'Well –' Geoff's head came up and he gazed at the clock – 'quarter to five, it's my tea-time, must get off home.'

Annie was bitterly disappointed. She was about to say she'd better be off as well, but Eunice was addressing her, and so she turned away and half watched Geoff executing his butterfly, which almost displaced half the water in the bath.

'Oh, he allus does that,' Eunice said. 'Likes showing off – I don't expect he gets much chance to anyway.'

'Why, is he married, then?' Annie asked.

'Oh no – not him. He lives with his mam, there's nothing

like that there. He's nice enough though – soft as a brush. You just have to let him play games, harmless all right.'

They swam side by side up to the deep end, chatting as they went.

'I get a lot of swimming in, you know,' Eunice remarked as they set off on the return swim. 'I've got this apartment at Tenerife – used to go there with me husband like before he passed on. As a matter of fact I'm off in a fortnight.'

'Oh, you lucky thing,' Annie said.

'Well, you can come as well if you want.'

'You don't mean it!'

'I do.'

Annie listened to the harsh voice and seemed to hear the surging of the 'Destiny Waltz'. This was it then, this was the start – after the Black Forest gateaux and burgers and chips and Les, there was going to be mauve Eunice and foreign travel.

'Ee, I can't get over it.' Annie spluttered as she missed her stroke, and went under gurgling.

'Steady up,' she heard Eunice saying.

'I'm that flustered.'

'That's all right, love, you're on!'

Got the Message

I KNEW HE'D BE THERE, and he was. The minute the wicket-gate swung open and I stepped out into the road, I saw him. He was sitting in his new white Sierra. My white bird, he called it. Its double spoilers curved up like fish fins. He couldn't come too close because the screws keep the whole stretch under closed-circuit TV and you can't park.

Getting out into the open air was that good I couldn't believe it. The wind rushed at my face. It made me laugh to think of the screw peering at the TV screen, watching him in his flash car. I was real proud to be walking over to it, opening the door and climbing in.

'Hi, lad,' he said. 'How are you, then, our Paul?'

I looked at him and I felt glad. He had this thick, straight black hair and he gelled it so it shone like dripping wellingtons. There were ragged patches of pink in his grainy cheeks, and he was wearing a navy-blue shadow-striped suit. Radio 1 was going full-belt and he drummed along with his fingers on the steering-wheel.

'Glad to be on the out,' I said.

'First, a little celebration.'

He was always celebrating. I couldn't remember a time when he wasn't. About him there was this larger-than-life feeling . . . he was big; he acted big . . . and it was overlaid with something like menace.

Well, he drove straight to this club he always visited when he was home.

'Hello, Eric,' they shouted, 'how are you then?'

The barmaids were making for him already. He had this way of grinning and showing white teeth and smoothing back his hair with one hand. I used to watch him as a kid. He was snakelike how he charmed people. All these other fellers at the bar had to wait because the girls had spotted him.

'Two pints of bitter, then, Eric, and two chasers.'

'Leanne, that's my little boy, Paul.'

'Hi, Paul!'

This blonde bird was giving me the eye over and I felt a fool – it was usually like that. He'd be there, bursting with life, and I'd feel his energy cancelling me out. The more he came on, the worse I got.

We sat down at a table. He lit up and sucked the fag smoke into himself. Even that was a kind of deep savouring – as though he wasn't going to let any of the enjoyment escape.

An old Elvis record was playing on the juke box, 'Love me Tender', and he hummed along and tapped the lighter in his thumb and index finger on the club table.

I saw him meet this bird's eye. They stared at each other a full minute.

'I s'll be back in a jiff, lad,' he said and got up.

Somehow I couldn't stop watching him, the way his shoulders punched the day and the curves of his legs filled his trousers.

I'd been put away for three years, and nothing had changed.

Sitting there listening to another Golden Oldie, I reached for his cigs, took one and lit up. His car keys were lying beside them. I fell to thinking of our Nick. Our Nick was more like my dad, no problem with him.

My dad had this passion for boxing. He'd boxed a lot himself and we had to follow suit. I've never been interested but he made us. Me and our Nick had to fight without gloves and go on until one knocked the other unconscious. Nothing else would satisfy him. Of course, me being younger, it was generally me who was flattened.

His eyes would glow afterwards, and I used to feel kind of useless and guilty because I could never make him proud of me.

Once when Nick was about twelve he'd sneaked Melissa,

the kid next door, up into our bedroom, and was messing about with her in bed. I expected when my dad walked in that he'd strap him at least . . . but no. He congratulated him and gave him a fiver.

You've come of age, lad, he said, come of age!

He was buying the bird a short and then he sat down opposite her. She couldn't take her eyes off him. I was a bit pissed off – I suppose I thought that just for once we might talk . . . him and me. We never have. He's always worked away, and when he's shown, it's been straight to the club or the boozer. There had to be a crowd round him, and if it wasn't that, then he'd be at home telling our Nick something, but mainly it 'ud be Sally whom my mam would send to him. He's always said she was his little girl – 'My girl,' he'd said, 'my girl . . .' and he'd almost croon, and have this singing light in his eyes.

I'd been imagining this day for three years. That much bird is a long time – I could see my life drifting by – but at the end of the tunnel there was always the light: one day I'd be out again.

I was just going to fetch another pint when the barmaid came to my table.

'From your dad,' she said. The beer glass stood before me with the light catching its amber tones and the froth peaking like whipped cream. I let the beer glide down my throat and shut my eyes.

GBH, that's what it nearly always was . . . GBH . . . I don't think I'm a naturally vicious type, it's something I've learnt. I see my dad's eyes gleaming . . . Go on . . . go on . . . hit him, then, hit him! Oh, you're yeller, yeller.

It was then that I looked up and saw our Sal coming towards me. Nobody would tell me anything about our Sal. All I knew was she'd left home whilst I was inside and hadn't been back. She hadn't written to me either and I was a bit hurt about that.

Sally's my twin and has thick, curly blonde hair. She'd got it shaved short now though and was wearing an old jacket and torn jeans. She looked like a lad.

Straight across she came. She must have spotted me right from the off.

'Hi, Paul . . . I heard you was out and you'd be in 'ere.'

'News travels fast . . . Hi, Sal.'

'How are you then?'

'Marvellous! Couldn't be better, could I?'

'No,' she said, looking at me.

'What about you then?'

'Oh, so-so . . .' She let her eyes flick away. She has this baby-doll face, kind of chubby and pink-cheeked, and her eyelashes are long and sandy.

'You never wrote us or owt, while I was inside, did you?'

'Nope,' she said, 'I was settlin' in . . . got my own flat, you know . . .'

'Yer, that's what they said. Is it all right, then?'

'Oh yes, great.'

'What are you drinking?'

'Bacardi Coke, Paul . . . ta.'

As I was returning from the bar, I was just in time to see my dad loping back.

'Here, Sal,' I said.

'Ta, thanks, love.'

'Hello there, stranger. Where have you sprung from?'

He was looking at her as he always did, only maybe a shade different from what I remembered. After time in nick you learn a lot of things about the way people look and about what they're really telling you.

'Down under.' She didn't look at him, not once. Her eyes were on her drink. I'd seen that look before, that way of concentrating on a drink . . .

'You could have told us where you was, couldn't you. Been avoiding us, haven't you?'

'Well,' I said, 'cheers everybody! Cheers! Life begins today!'

'So, where've you been?'

'Around . . . Cheers, Paul.' She turned and smiled at me and I could see her lips were quivering.

He had shaken out another cig and was lighting up and

drawing down the smoke inside him. All his movements were very precise and well-practised and kind of mesmerizing. Sal was watching his hands tapping the lighter on the table. He wasn't liking how she was holding out, I could tell, and I noticed I was forgetting to breathe and my shoulders were tensed.

It was like being in the showers, feeling the jets of tepid water sliding down your face and wondering if someone would glide a blade between your ribs before you came out. It was easy in the showers . . . or they might get you at slopping-out, first off.

She had finished her drink.

'Bacardi Coke?' he said, and she nodded and he went to order more drinks.

When he came back with the orders, he fixed on her again. It was just like old times at home with his bad moods rippling through the house like a draught. Doors banged. Somebody was screaming. It might have been because Sal had stayed out late or had cut off all her hair and had this butterfly tattoo done on her arm; or it might have been the telly channels; or just the way he was. He liked things to be happening, people around all the time, and when it went quiet his bad moods would growl in him: The dinner's crap, always the same . . .

'You used to look such a beautiful little girl,' he said, and his voice deepened and I saw the singing in his eyes again, just for a fraction of a second.

'Oh yer,' she croaked and her face went dead white. Her hands trembled as she made herself a roll-up, she wouldn't touch his cigs.

Sal's the one I think most of in the family. I've a lot of time for her. And it came to me as I listened that I'd missed something somewhere; during all those years at home before I first got put away at sixteen, something had gone wrong.

'Why do you have to wear them crap clothes? What's a matter with you?'

How her right hand holding the roll-up shook!

'I'm what you made me,' she said.

I could hardly hear her voice. On the juke box Mick Jagger screamed about getting no satisfaction.

I listened to the voice and drained my pint and I heard another voice, my mam's: Sal, go and give your dad a cuddle, go on, love . . . go and give him a cuddle . . . there's only you can bring him round.

He was rambling on about other girls and how nicely they dressed and how she looked a slag. Her eyes were like glass, and then one of the barmaids came over.

'Eric,' she said, 'Diane over there's been trying to attract your attention for ages.'

'Thanks, love,' he said, but before he could move, Sal jumped straight up and left, just like that. I could feel this pounding in my ears.

'Back in a minute, Paul,' he said, and shot off to the bird's table.

I just sat there and remembered how it was him who'd got me put away the first time for drawing a couple of grand with his credit card, and then I glanced at his keys. They were still there by his cig packet and his drink. He looked across as I picked them up and swung them round my index finger.

'Eh!'

'Yer?' I said.

The bird was smiling at me, trying to impress him with what pull she had.

'What you doin' with my keys?'

'Goin' after our Sal.'

'No, not with my car you aren't.'

It all came on me then in that split second as I looked into his eyes that were swimmy and mean.

'Oh yes I am,' I said. 'And while I'm at it, that's for screwin' our Sal.' And I lunged straight across the table and slapped him about the mouth. He went all rigid like a dummy and toppled over backwards. The bird was screaming and beer was spuming all over the place.

Whilst they were goggling with their mouths open, I cleared off.

The Sierra stood on the pub car park, its fins rising, its bodywork immaculate . . . his white bird. I unlocked it, slid in behind the wheel, turned on the ignition, did a rev or two, and I was away.

It was then that I knew there are some things you can never write off, ever . . .

Absence Makes the Heart Grow Fonder

GEMMA HAD BEEN LOOKING for true love all her life. She couldn't remember when she had first heard about it – it might have been in her mam's magazines, because mam had been reading *Woman's Weekly* for years. Gemma had sat in the kitchen after school turning the pages showing knitting patterns and fashions and new recipes to reach the illustrations of handsome, dark-haired men, often doctors, about to kiss young nurses. The nurses' eyes would be wide open and their lips parted in ecstasy. This was what she wanted; nothing else would do.

And now, suddenly, she had found her true love and was going to meet him for the first time. Radio 1 gurgled away and she hummed along and waltzed to and fro.

She was dribbling articles into a flight bag: a new and exotic piece of lingerie – a black teddy – some black satin knickers and a suspender belt.

The doors of her gold and white built-in wardrobe stood open and Gemma stared at the line of dresses and skirts hanging there. She supposed she would wear the blue suit and the white satin blouse, although she had a longing for something more alluring. When she'd worn black ski pants and a rather revealing silver top to a disco in town, Mandy, her sixteen-year-old daughter, had screwed up her face and said:

Mam, you're never going out in that, are you?

Gemma had felt her confidence crumbling. She loved romance – valentine cards, and presents tied with bows of scarlet ribbon; bunches of carnations; single red roses; 'Love Is' stickers; pictures of kittens and puppies, and small children with big eyes. And her taste in clothes was similar – she went in for pussycat bows and silky material and her stilettos were five inches high. That was why it always took her a long time to reach anywhere. She would clop along slowly, swaying from the hips and listening to her personal stereo which clung to her ears under furry pale-blue ear-muffs.

Yes, it would have to be the baby-blue suit – she couldn't afford to buy anything new and that was a pity. If Des had paid up, it would have been different, but he wouldn't. She'd tried to get him for maintenance for the three kids but had never succeeded. Des was her ex. How wrong can you be about people! She had met Des when she was seventeen.

Should she take the special-offer fluffy pink hand-towel? But surely hotels were meant to have towels of their own, weren't they? She didn't know, because she'd never stayed in one.

If Des hadn't . . . She had been working on Binns perfumery counter at the time and Des had stood staring at her. He'd been very handsome with crisp black hair and his pale badger stripe and he'd worn a dark suit and he'd made her think of magazine doctors.

Got Chanel Number 5, have you, love?

Yes, sir.

Just the way he'd said 'love' had set her in a quiver.

She'd placed the white boxes on the counter, touching them with the tips of her long red nails. In those days she'd been a very thin, white-blonde girl with big blue eyes. Now she was a bit curvy – she studied her hips in the dressing-table mirror – and her hair had to be helped on a bit and blobbed about her face like balls of cotton wool. Still an' all . . .

She'd looked at Des and she'd thought: Here he is, this is my true love . . .

Who could be getting the Chanel? she'd wondered – largest size too. He'd kept coming into the store after that, and would stand and watch her, half smiling. She'd been unable to sleep at night with the suspense of it. This must be true love. She hadn't known his name or what he did. His hands were big and red and rough and didn't seem to match his dark suit, but that had been only a little thing.

For two months he'd disappeared – every day she'd hoped to see him, but he'd never come into the store again. And then one day, quite suddenly, he'd been standing there gazing at her. He'd wooed her with boxes of Black Magic and bottles of scent and he'd taken her to steak houses and been very persuasive.

But somehow after she'd become pregnant with Tom and they'd got married real quick and he'd been off on his oil-rig for months on end, things had changed. He'd come home loaded but, within three days, the money would have been splurged – either on dogs or horses or expensive presents. After the spending would come the drinking and he'd black her eyes and loosen her teeth and once he'd broken her ribs. And for sure that wasn't true love.

The end had been when he'd had the electric organ installed and he'd sat down and tried to pump out 'I'll Be Loving You Eternally', and the house had vibrated and next-doors had come round knocking to complain.

It was then that she'd taken the three kiddies to her mam's. After that she'd been quite ill, it had got to her heart somehow.

She didn't want to remember anything about the past . . . Well, most of the time she didn't think of it, because she was writing to Wayne Pendrill and he was her true love. Since knowing Wayne Pendrill her life had changed, it had swooped and soared. She liked to think of how it had all started.

Her friend Denise had been writing to penfriends for years, and one day when Gemma had been complaining about the stupid men she met at Lexington Avenue, who only wanted to get into bed with her, Denise had said:

What you want is a penpal. I'll bring my magazine round and you can write to a feller in there – get somebody in the USA – they'll be rich at least.

Yes, she'd said, I'm just sick of them stupid lads at the Lexington – they're either trying to get their hands into your tights or they're throwing up on you. I get fed up with it . . .

not my idea of a night out . . . I've just had to have my white cat-suit dry-cleaned . . .

That was how she'd come to write to Wayne Pendrill. Now, at first she'd been a bit worried about how to word her letters. She'd been good at English at school and had liked writing and making up stories – in fact once she'd won a prize for the best story in her class, but that had been a long time ago.

Lend us your dictionary, Eddy, there's a love, she'd asked her youngest, who was still at school.

She'd bought herself a thick pad of blue Basildon Bond airmail paper and she'd started:

> Dear Mr Pendrill,
>
> I understand you are looking for a penfriend. My name is Gemma Scott and I am 39 years old. [She'd decided that when she'd reached thirty-nine, she wouldn't get any older.] I am divorced with three children, Tom, Mandy, Eddy. What are your hobbies? Mine are music – I like the Golden Oldies – you know, Elvis, Frank Sinatra, Nat King Cole. I like discos and reading – particularly Mills and Boonses. I like writing too. You'll gather from this that I am an old-fashioned girl. My birth-sign is Scorpio. I know that's supposed to have a sting in its tail but I'm not like that. What is your birth-sign?
>
> Oh I am a non-smoker. I love animals and children and films that make you cry.
>
> Yours faithfully
> Mrs Gemma Scott

His first letter, like all the subsequent ones, had been written on thick white paper. The handwriting was big and looped and very dramatic. He'd used pen and black ink and not a blue biro like she had. Just the sight of his strong, curving letters impressed her. She'd stared and stared at them.

Dear Gemma,

Oh, God, he'd put 'Dear Gemma', not 'Dear Mrs Scott'!

Dear Gemma,

Hello, penfriend, I just know this is going to be the start of a beautiful friendship. Let me introduce myself to you.

I am forty, a divorced businessman with two kids, Wayne Junior, twelve, and Maybelle, fourteen.

You ask about my hobbies. I guess they're listening to music, baseball, movies, theater, travel.

You sound the cutest little woman. What about sending me a photo?

She'd read the letter over and over – twice before going out to the shops to buy the beefburgers and frozen chips for dinner, and six times after she'd returned. She became nervous at the idea of sending a photograph of herself . . . nor did she really want to see one of him. It somehow spoiled the purity of the relationship . . . besides, she hated having her photograph taken. She wanted to remain how she was in her head; anything else would be too distracting.

The kids thought it was a joke when the letters started arriving. They couldn't understand the magic of it. When the letter-box flap clappered, Gemma would go pelting downstairs in her pale-blue leisure suit to retrieve the letter. Her heart would be pattering and bumping . . . Would it be? Or was it some boring old bill or a rubbish-mail drop? When it was a letter from Wayne, she'd rush into the kitchen, switch on the electric kettle, make herself a coffee, and then take the letter back to the front room. On the tape-deck she'd put 'Songs for Lovers' and then, snuggled on the carpet before the imitation log-fire, she would slit the letter open carefully with a knife and read on . . .

I have this picture of you as being real fragile, a somebody who needs looking after. You are real sensitive, that's for sure. One day I hope I shall show you this great country, the States, and maybe you will introduce me to the home country. My grandparents were from somewhere called Blackburn – maybe you know that place?

When I'm writing to you, Gemma, I feel like I'm talking to you – it's like you're sitting here with me.

She always wrote back immediately. In fact she became so busy answering his letters that there wasn't even time to go disco dancing at Lexington Avenue. Instead she'd put the tape for lovers on the deck, turn up the electric fire and have the logs glowing with threads of light and write by the pinky gleam of the reading lamp. From upstairs would come the panting and thumping of heavy metal as Eddy and friends enjoyed themselves.

This was true love. She had to look up words like *receive* in Eddy's dictionary because she could never remember about the *i* and the *e* or whether you put another *e* in sincerely, and she didn't want Wayne to think she was a dumbo.

It had started with one letter a week, and then it progressed to two a week, and finally one arrived every day.

She pictured this tall, dark-haired man with a touch of grey at his temples, and big dark eyes, misty with emotion. He seemed to be there all the time. In fact she got into the habit of talking to him in her head.

Dearest Wayne,

Today in the supermarket there was this madwoman, she was nattering away to herself and I thought what a terrible life to be mad like that and to have nobody. You see, she is often in there – I've seen her before and she always wears the same awful raincoat – never changes. What we all want is a bit of love. It's what I've been looking for always, you know. Mandy doesn't understand how I feel about you. She goes out with this dreadful boy who wears leathers and has a motorbike. You ask if she is dating – well, yes – he is the one. He is a mechanic. I

> would like her to know a better class of person, but there it is . . . Such people don't know what love is.

She no longer wrote 'Yours faithfully' or 'Yours sincerely' but 'Love', 'Love Gemma'. The first time his letter said 'All my love', she let herself drop splat on the three-piece suite and listened to the rhumba of her heart. 'All my love' – this tall, distinguished man was writing this to her from all those miles away. His words, written with black ink on thick, expensive paper, were more important than any words which might have been spoken. They were like the Ten Commandments engraved on the tablets of white stone.

> You are all I ever dreamt of . . . you are the sweetest, gentlest, cutest girl I know . . . I have been looking for you all my life, and now I've found you . . .

Gemma moved in a trance. She didn't even get irritated with Eddy's heavy metal vibrating the ceiling and the ceiling-rose threatening to come thumping down. Nor did she shriek about the smell of cigarette smoke in the bedrooms.

She was listening to Wayne's deep, dark voice whispering to her.

And then the letter had arrived.

> My Darling Gemma,
>
> I hope to come to dear old England – what say we meet at Heathrow and spend a weekend together? I can't wait for your reply – though I guess I'm a shy man and just the thought of seeing you has gotten me into quite a state . . .

Coming to Heathrow . . . weekend in London! Suddenly everything had begun to revolve faster and faster. She was spinning . . . How could they manage to meet? How could she bear it? She felt like she'd done when she'd read a book and then gone to see the film of it . . .

His last letter had said:

Honey, I'm on my way . . . I guess our meeting is going to be the most important thing that's ever happened to me . . . I can't wait . . .

The most important thing that ever happened!

She kept pausing in mid-trot from dressing-table to flight bag and falling into a dream. This was like nothing ever before . . . and the fact that there had once been the awful flash Harry, Des Scott, and the maintenance battles, and the black eyes and broken ribs, and since then the spewings-up and the little lechings at Lexington Avenue, made the moment more breathtakingly precious. It was like some Christmas snowflake suspended dazzlingly in a black sky.

'Love is Wayne Pendrill' she wrote in scarlet lipstick across her dressing-table mirror, and then she did a wowy lipstick kiss at the side of the second *l* and gazed at the imprint of her lips and the way it was stippled with little lines.

All the way to London on the train she sat very upright in her baby-blue suit. Her face was powdered white but there was delicate pink blusher on the cheekbones and her lips were candy pink, and her nails matched. Her blue eye-shadow toned with the speedwell blue of her eyes and her stilettos were bright blue too.

Every hour she tinkled off to the ladies to freshen up her make-up and spray on some Je Reviens that Tom had bought her for her last birthday – Tom was going to be like his dad, she suspected. She stood in the ladies as the train lurched and ground to a halt, fluffing out her blonde cotton-wool hair about her cheeks.

What would she say when she saw him? They were both to wear pink carnations in their lapels.

She'd brought a romance to read but she couldn't get into it, because what was happening to her seemed more enthralling and more romantic than anything in the story.

He would come walking towards her down a long shining vista and then they would begin to run and finally they would embrace.

'This your guard speaking. We are now approaching London King's Cross,' a confidential Asian voice murmured, and that too seemed part of the magic.

There was a disgusting smell of burning brake linings as the InterCity slowed and pulled up. Everybody began to bundle out. Gemma took her time. She never hurried. Personal stereo in place, she clopped steadily down the platform towards the barrier. Tom had told her it would take an hour to reach Heathrow. The tension was by turns unbearable and then pleasant. The journey had been going on for a hundred years – she had started as a young girl and now she was a middle-aged woman with a weak heart.

Heathrow amazed her. It was a huge, confusing place tracked by hundreds of escalators, and there were giant boards plotting the arrivals and departures of aeroplanes, winking lights and voices saying, 'Last call now for New York.' 'Last call for Düsseldorf.' 'Flight BA 1642 now boarding.'

It was like being in another country. Brown men in long white nightshirts and with their heads swathed in white cloths moved in groups and flapped their hands; doe-eyed creatures in saris and with clinking gold bracelets clutched babies and wheeled push-chairs. There were people such as she'd never ever seen before in her life, all flowing forward, and she was caught up in them.

Then the words on the arrivals board hit her. The Pan Am jumbo jet had already arrived. She peered round in the crush of bodies and the approaching luggage trolleys which could plough you down and trundle over you without noticing.

She felt very small all of a sudden. Amongst the exquisite young girls with smooth brown faces and dangling gold earrings and the confident students in their skin-tight leggings and body-stockings she was an aged matron. There was nothing zingy or eye-stopping in her appearance – whereas alone in her bedroom she had been tingling with energy and radiance.

Where was he? Where was that shining vista? And then she saw the small, rather plump-looking man in the cowboy hat and check shirt who was lashed about with cameras. Beside him squatted an enormous flight bag. He had a pink carnation in his button-hole.

No, she thought, no, it can't be . . . this must be someone else.

She was hidden from his view by a stall selling fresh orange. A queue formed constantly at it as people waited to receive polystyrene cups of juice. Should she go back down the tube station and pretend she'd not seen him?

But he'd come all that way . . . no, that would be wrong . . . all that way . . . was it six hours by plane? Perhaps it wouldn't be Wayne, and then she could feel relieved and continue searching. She cleared her throat, and emerged from behind the stall.

'Er . . . excuse me . . . would you be, er . . . you aren't Mr Wayne Pendrill by any chance?'

He began to smile. He had perfect teeth.

'Woll, I sure am pleased to meet you. It's got to be Gemma!'

Gemma found her hand being grasped and pumped in a formal sort of way, but with exuberance. She felt acutely embarrassed and blushed.

'Oh, hello, very pleased to meet you . . . I hadn't realized the plane had come . . . it's very busy, isn't it . . . I mean, and most confusing.'

'It sure is . . . You look kinda flustered?'

'Well, I'm not used to . . . er . . .'

'Sure, maybe we should make for the elevator and get into the subway . . . or whatever?'

'Yes.'

She couldn't believe that she was going to spend the weekend with this weird little bloke. She wished she could have caught the InterCity straight back, but there was clearly no way of escape.

'Gee, this bag's sure heavy!'

'Yes, it looks it. Did you have a pleasant journey?' Had they really written all those things to each other? Had he said: You are all I ever dreamt of . . . ? Could he really have written those words on that lovely paper? If only he didn't wear that awful hat! Mandy would say: Cor, what a nerk! Mam, you won't go with him, will you? She could imagine their faces. Tom would open his mouth wide and laugh until he coughed. You can't be serious . . . God, Mam, you don't mean it!

'We'll take a cab straight there once we hit London.'

Gemma was thankful for the press of bodies which prevented their speaking to each other.

They were going through the glass swing-doors into the hotel and Gemma felt as though she was in a daze.

'I kinda booked these two rooms with adjoining doors – I hope that's all right with you, Gemma?'

He was looking into her face and smiling, but seriously, and when she studied his features they were quite pleasant and good humoured and she liked them.

'Oh, that's fine by me.'

'I hoped it would be.'

'Yes,' she said, not wanting to think of the white satin nightdress with the thin shoulder-straps which she had put in her bag.

'Well,' he said, 'I think I should freshen up a bit . . . Will I see you down in the bar?'

'Oh yes, that would be fine.' She was relieved at this.

With the interconnecting door closed, she sat on the bed and tried to relax. The room was all beige and cream and there was a long window draped in white nets, and beyond it she could see a wrought-iron balcony. Everything that was happening seemed to be cutting her off from her dreaming side; it was as though she had advanced into another world – it didn't even appear to be the *real* world. It did in fact possess a disconcerting unreality about it. She kept wondering if she had fallen asleep and was dreaming.

She changed into a silky flowered sheath dress and renewed her make-up carefully, then she clopped off in search of the bar.

Hardly had she sat down and he was there. Without the awful cowboy hat he seemed quite normal, and she didn't have to keep glancing about her, wondering what other people in their vicinity were making of it, and whether or not they were laughing at him.

He fetched her a sherry and he had a G and T.

'Do we take in a movie tonight?' he asked her when they had both had a good gulp at their drinks.

'Oh yes, why not . . . that sounds a nice idea!'

'Gee . . . do you realize, ma'am, this is my first time in London . . . London, this great ole city! Houses of Parliament, Buckingham Palace . . . gee . . . I sure do want to see everything!'

She giggled, feeling the waves of his enthusiasm bowling towards her. That was how he was: little, indomitable and endlessly enthusiastic.

'Well, I've only seen them once myself – school trip when I was a kid.'

'That right? I've promised my kids see . . . photos of everything!'

'Yes, well, I suppose it makes it a bit different . . .'

'Different from what?'

'Oh, I was just saying.'

He gave her a grin and showed his white teeth, and the laughter lines fanned about his eyes.

'England . . . gee . . . can't believe it!'
His brown eyes were shining. 'Here I am in the middle of London having drinks with this English lady!'

'I'm not really a lady,' Gemma murmured modestly.

They went into the nearest cinema and saw *Ghost*, which forced Gemma to concentrate on her mascara in order to prevent herself from crying.

'Did you enjoy the movie?' he asked afterwards.

'Oh yes, except it made me want to cry.'

'But you like a good cry?' His eyes were twinkling at her and she managed not to think about his cowboy hat.

They ate prawn cocktail, chicken Maryland and french fries, asparagus spears and great wedges of Black Forest gateau, which they encouraged with champagne.

'The old country – this is where they came from all that time ago – think about that – maybe we could take in Blackburn as well?'

'Oh, that's miles away – besides you'd not find it very interesting – I think it's just industrial.'

He seemed to think that you could just go buzzing about as though in a helicopter; he didn't have any clues about British Rail and all the complications of travel and delays and waitings on platforms.

She half listened as he exclaimed in wonder at the quaintness of everything, and felt herself being borne along by his energy. This foreign country amazed her too.

In a state of intoxication brought about by much champagne-drinking and his constant caperings, she managed to clop along to her room. As though enchanted by this little ole country and his fine white teeth chomping on everything, she fell into bed, knocked out, and slept until she heard a tap on the door and shot upright in bed.

'Gemma, Gemma, you ready for breakfast?'

'No . . . no, Wayne, not yet . . . I'll, er . . . meet you downstairs.'

'Okay, honey!'

The battering of his energy receded and she was able to grope out of bed, aware that maybe she had drunk rather a lot the night before.

That day they did stand before the gates of Buckingham Palace and he shot reel after reel of film and exclaimed at the guards' headgear.

'Gee, that's some hat! Bet he doesn't get cold ears! Say, do you get tired standing there like that?'

Gemma's ankles swelled up and she'd find herself way behind Wayne's onward march, but then he would come panting back and grinning, with the cowboy hat perched at a drunken angle.

'This is some country, ma'am . . . some country!'

'Glad you're enjoying it.'

'Aren't you, then, Gemma honey?'

He looked suddenly wistful and Gemma couldn't bear it

and she agreed that it was all marvellous and fascinating and she'd never had such a good time in her life before.

'Just hold it there, honey . . . yes . . . like that . . . with that cute little smile . . . yes . . .'

Click and the shutter went and he was preparing to snap something else.

After the Tower of London and Madame Tussaud's, they came to a halt. Gemma knew she had sore heels and probably a corn on each little toe.

Saturday night they sat long over dinner, drinking more champagne as they cut up their french fries and steak, and Wayne looked around for some suitable sauce in which to smother the steak and finally settled on tomato ketchup. Whilst smacking the bottom of the bottle, he proved too vigorous and the bottle gobbed up a dollop of red stuff on the cloth. By this time Gemma wasn't even remotely embarrassed.

Something had happened, Gemma caught herself realizing, whenever she emerged for a fraction of a second from Wayne's casual burblings, and the jog and blunder of their conversation. It pulled her with it and submerged her. She found herself speculating on all manner of things about which she would never in a hundred years have thought. He would keep referring to her; asking her things . . . and then: You don't say, Gemma. Say, what do you make of that? And how did *you* take that?

All as though he were conducting some kind of interview, and she thought: He really wants to know about me. And she told him about Des and the maintenance struggles and about thinking she'd got milk-bottle legs so she never liked men to walk upstairs after her in buses. That made him smile and crinkle up his eyes and say, 'Gee, Gemma, you've got the nicest pair of legs I've ever seen!'

And then, before she had really thought, it was Sunday and he was leaving for Heathrow and she was bound for the InterCity back home.

'Say, Gemma, this sure was a great weekend.'

'Yes,' she said, 'it was.'

They were waiting for their taxis to arrive. He was sitting opposite her, wearing one of his loud check shirts that reflected on his face and seemed to make his cheeks even redder, and he was grinning. She was nervous and her stomach churned. They had not even kissed. Why they hadn't, she couldn't say, but the connecting door had remained resolutely closed.

'Taxis,' the hotel porter announced and they rose at the same time.

'Gee, Gemma . . . this was really some weekend . . . Bye now!'

And he was in his taxi and already disappearing and all she could make out of him was the mole hill of his cowboy hat in the rear windscreen.

In a great rush she was overcome by sadness, by a feeling of being bereft. She missed the chivvying nasal exhortations: Say, Gemma. Gee, did you *see* that! The blocks of the old country were gradually heaving back into place. She did not know where she had been. But now there was this sense of loss . . . and she was not at all clear why that was.

As she sat in the InterCity a letter began forming in her head.

> Dearest Wayne,
>
> This weekend was the happiest time of my life. You showed me that many things my head's just rocking with them . . . I . . .

She couldn't wait to get home and write the most beautiful letter she had ever written. It would flow along. Tears ran down her cheeks as she thought of it, causing mascara dribbles to form thick black runnels on the white powdered surface.

Wayne Pendrill, she said to herself, Wayne Pendrill, I shall write some wonderful, wonderful letters . . .

Elsie's Revenge

Later, after the awful event had passed, Elsie Grantham was to reflect that sometimes when you fire a bolt you might miss the target but hit something even more worthwhile.

First thing one morning, when she was wondering what to do about her suspension from work, the phone pinged. Elsie grabbed it. She didn't like phones. She preferred to see people's faces when they were addressing her – that way you knew if they were pulling a stroke.

'Oh, er . . . Miss Cartwright here, Mrs Grantham, er . . . Mr Smith asked me to say we shan't be needing your services any longer.'

Click. Click, just like that! 'Miss Cartright,' Elsie snorted, 'Miss pratting Cartright!' She pictured Julie, the office bottle, stilettoing round after Smitho and simpering Yes, Mr Smith, no, Mr Smith . . . giggle, giggle. Shall I get you a coffee?

Now, from the first moment when Smitho had taken over in her section, Elsie had sensed that he was one of those who regard cleaners as the lowest form of life – especially if they happen to be well over thirty with a 'nearly new' face. Of course there were scabs like her fellow cleaner, Mavis, who pandered to him. She in her way was as bad as the office bottle. She would put on her girly voice:

Oh, Mr Smith . . . you don't say . . . is that right . . . And Smitho would kink back his hair with one hand, tuck his chin in and give a little preeny smile.

But when it came to her, it was: You've not cleaned that floor very well, Elsie. I hope you don't call that finished!

Well, if you bring the muck in on it when it's damp, what do you expect?

He would frazzle her with one of his flame-thrower glares.

Anyway, little by little it had been getting worse at work. Elsie remembered how she used to love waking up in the morning with the thought of her cleaning in front of her. Cleaning was her escape. She cleaned her husband, Dermot, out of her system. It hadn't been so bad when he'd been away at sea, but since he got made redundant there'd been hours and hours of family fun. He was a loomer and whatever she was doing he'd be hovering and inspecting, and then it would be Elsie, where's my dinner? or Elsie, what do you call this? Them's not peas – they're bullets more like . . . and what am I supposed to do with this, eh? Where's the meat?

Nothing was ever right: there were creases on his shirts and You've not ironed this . . . oh, I'll not wear this!

One shirt would be screwed up in a ball and hurled into a corner. She hated ironing and could never get it right. When you'd finished with the front, there'd be great lines and rucks on the back. It was enough to make you scream.

Sometimes they even had boxing matches, not that she landed any punches.

As soon as she arrived at work, Elsie would fill her bucket with sparkly water, get down on her hands and knees in a corner and scrub. She always had her own scrubbing-brush and red plastic bucket. The bristles scrabbling in circles along the tiles tore Dermot to fragments of skin and bone, or dumped him in a gigantic mincer which shredded him until he was a big red lump of goo.

Even such exercises had been forbidden. Gauleiter Smith had stopped her on the fateful morning.

'Elsie, for goodness' sake, we provide machines for washing floors. What do you think you're doing – wasting time?'

But the crisis hadn't come then. It had happened later that day.

Mavis, who had absented herself for three weeks, supposedly suffering from backache but really gobbling burgers and chips on the Costa Brava, had resurfaced. After all the clubby nights and roasting days she was really in top form, batting her eyelashes and wiggling her bottom at Smitho.

'Oh, I can't do any bending, Mr Smith . . . not with *my* back.'

'What a shame, love . . .' He'd given Mavis a nudge and a wink. 'We'll put you on light duties, for now . . . Elsie, you go on the polisher when you've finished with the floor-washer.'

When he was busy burbling away about the glories of the Hoovermatic washing-machine, the row had erupted.

'You look well leaving me with all this, Mave,' Elsie had muttered, 'particularly seein' as I've had double to do while you've been away.'

Mavis had smirked and wiggled off.

'Eh up, I'm talking to you . . .'

'Oh, Elsie, you do go on . . . always whingeing.'

'Whingeing, am I? You go and piss off!' Elsie didn't realize how her voice was screeching, or that her right arm had risen of its own accord to clout Mavis. All the people peering at electrical gadgets suddenly nebbed at her. She saw their eyes round with shock.

Smitho said, 'Do excuse me!' and came striding up. He loomed over her. It was just like Dermot and she expected to receive a clatter round the ear. His lips were jammed close together and the words hissed out. 'I can't have this kind of behaviour in here, Elsie, you are suspended as from now. Go and get your coat on!'

Trembling with rage, Elsie had dragged her anorak off the peg and pulled it on over her overall, then she'd seized her bucket and scrubbing-brush and crashed off to fetch the bike.

On the way home all manner of curses had blasted out of her. What was she going to do next?

All night long she'd listened to Dermot snuffling in his nose and had lain rigid with fury and uncertainty. What would happen now? Dermot's response had been:

'Oh, it's your own fault . . . you had it coming . . . I've told you . . .' Dermot, of course, always *knew*.

Now that the office bottle Cartright's phone call had come, everything was quite clear. The first shot had been fired.

Elsie stood glaring at the telephone and breathed in deeply. She was trembling with rage like she had been the previous day. Well, this time Smitho was going to pay. Muttering to herself, she blundered into the kitchen and opened the cupboard under the sink where she kept her precious cleaning things. On this occasion she wouldn't be able to go on her bike, it would have to be the bus.

At the door she paused, bucket in hand, and listened; no, there wasn't a sound from upstairs. Dermot had been having a bevvy the night before, a usual occurrence, and wouldn't lumber down until afternoon.

She'd disguised the bucket in a huge plastic carrier-bag so that nobody would cotton on to what she was about. Every time the bus lurched, she inspected it to see that none of its precious contents was being spilled. Whenever she ran through the scene in her head, she found herself starting to grin.

There'd be Smitho in his navy-blue pin-striped suit, mincing about like a streak of lightning round the machines.

'Now, Modom, can I interest you in the new Hoovermatic . . . ?' And as he closed the washing-machine door and flicked the buttons, she would pour the bucket of water over his head, and he'd come up blinking, like some sea-creature, all his careful hair flattened to his skull, and she'd croak in his ear:

'You can keep your bloody job, Smitho!'

And she'd hare off before any of them could catch her. Smitho 'ud have to be given cups of tea by the handmaidens and be taken home to dry off after his ordeal. With any luck his suit might have shrunk too.

By the time she reached the store, she was sweating and trembling. She couldn't think of any time in her life when she had actually triumphed . . . but this time she must. It wasn't merely Smitho she would be flattening; in some curious way, she felt it would also be Dermot. Well, Dermot never believed she could pull anything off.

It was a very well-bred store with lots of gleaming chrome and glass. In the big plate-glass display windows automatic washing-machines, dish-washers, vacuum cleaners and split-level ovens were standing, all washed in a pale pink light. Prices were discreet.

Elsie went round to the back, to the goods entrance where there was the staff door used by porters and cleaners.

Nobody saw her. Her heart clanged and she had to stand still for a while because she was breathing in great gulps. Bank robbers must feel like this, she thought, or assassins with crossbows or guns.

A couple of sparkies were messing with some electrical wiring but they didn't even turn round as she passed them. She was invisible, she knew that, and had been all her life – one of those people whom eyes never register.

Before her was Smitho's room. What would she say if someone asked what she was up to? Cleaning? But she had been sacked. Never mind. They wouldn't know.

She turned the handle and the door opened. Would he be in there, sitting at his desk? In fact the room was empty. It smelt of air freshener. That cow Mavis would have given it a bottoming during the morning. Perhaps he'd be out front . . . well, so much the better!

Elsie strode out amongst the graciously positioned islands of merchandise. A silky tune was playing. Customers meandered to and fro, faces puckered with concentration. The buying of electric gadgets was a very important matter.

He was nowhere to be seen, but she caught sight of Mavis scurrying off in the direction of the under-manager's office. The next thing she knew, this floor-walker was ushering her back to Smitho's room.

'Where's Smitho?' she asked him.

'Who was you wanting?'

'Mr Smith.'

'He's not about at the moment – you've to stay in here.' With that he locked her in. She couldn't believe it. Her heart boomed and skipped and she felt all hot and strange. Her bucket of water stood beside her. She sat down on Smitho's black plastic swivel-chair and swung madly to and fro for several intoxicating moments – she had never dared to do that before. Then she fiddled with his biros for a bit and wrote 'E. G. woz here' like they used to do in the changing cubicles at the baths and in the lavs when she was a kid.

After what seemed years, the door was unlocked and a policeman was ushered in by the under-manager and followed by the floor-walker with a walkie-talkie and another heavy.

'Now, what's all this about?' the policeman asked.

'What's what about?'

'I understand you no longer work here.'

'That's what Smitho said.'

'Well, what are you doing here – this is trespass, you know – and what's the bucket of water for?'

'Smitho, for his head.'

'Do I understand you were wanting to carry out an assault on Mr Smith's person?'

Why couldn't he talk to her properly? she wondered. Misery was making her feel quite weak.

'Oh, I don't know.'

The copper rambled on a bit, said he was cautioning her and he hoped there'd be no more of this sort of caper, otherwise she'd be in proper trouble, and he gave further dire warnings.

'Well, you'd better let us empty that.'

He was about to motion to one of the heavies to take her bucket.

'No,' she said, 'no, that's mine, that's my water.'

That made the copper laugh.

'You're a funny woman, Mrs Grantham,' he said.

They all ushered her out of the store and watched as she trudged off with her bucket. She could feel their eyes sending poison darts into her back.

Whatever happened she wouldn't ever reveal her disgrace to Dermot. If she hurried up, she'd be back even before he staggered downstairs. They'd have fish fingers, beans and chips for dinner but she'd have to be quick. He'd have his mouth open waiting for the worm like the baby sparrows she'd watched in the yard.

Elsie had the fat frizzling in the chip-pan and was poking the bubbling beans when she heard a great crash behind her.

Dermot was spreadeagled on the floor, having tumbled over her bucket. Water swam about the kitchen floor.

'Me leg . . . me leg . . . You daft bitch . . . look what you've done . . . why didn't you . . . ? I can't get up . . . Give us a hand up then!'

She had to haul him into a sitting position but he couldn't rise.

'Listen 'ere . . . I must have broke me leg.'

As Elsie dialled 999 and asked for an ambulance she was feeling almost cheerful and could murmur soothing sounds to Dermot in his suffering.

A Picture of You

WITH MICHELLE BEING my best mate, I've found this whole thing very difficult to get over.

Right from the off it seemed a very weird day. There'd been nothing but shots of planes on telly and monster tanks rumbling along; a line of camels humping by flapping their eyelids, and the odd palm tree and a few explosions. The kiddies had got bored with it and Kelly had been into everything and emptied Daz and Comfort all over the kitchen floor. Anyway, I'd decided we'd go round to Michelle's mam's to see her, being as she'd rung up to say Michelle was visiting.

I was a bit excited about being with her again. We used to have such great times together, but it all seemed a long time ago – not that it was really, except my life has changed and that's what made it like a century since it all happened.

We were just passing Barclays Bank when I noticed this big navy-blue van with the metal mesh and bars on the window.

Sheralee said, 'Mam, what does it say in the letters?'

'Securicor Cares,' I said.

Then I saw him get out. He's six foot and always walks as though he's on parade and his black shoes gleam. You couldn't see his hair – that's shaved real close to his skull – because he was wearing a navy-blue helmet with a vizor thing on it.

We came face to face. He couldn't miss me. It made me feel real odd. I haven't set eyes on him for a couple of years. Kelly had been a baby when he'd cleared off. Sheralee didn't know who he was either. Only the older ones would have maybe recognized him.

He just nodded at me and I nodded back. And then it came

up in my head just like a neon sign: I was married to him. He was my husband – husband for seven years.

It had started like a dream. Me and Michelle had gone to Romeos one Saturday night and there were these two soldiers, Dean and Barry. Dean's a fantastic dancer, or used to be until he got his foot crushed. He looked at me. I was standing talking to Michelle and I saw this chap staring. It made me feel weak. I never heard a word she said. I was just looking at her but not listening. I knew *he* was concentrating on me. It made my face go cold, but I didn't give anything away – nobody would have known.

That night went on and on but I thought: If he doesn't speak to me soon, I'll scream. I can't bear it. Everything seemed to be going on for years and years – just him staring at me, and me pretending I didn't know. He was that big and strong and caring . . . somehow. His eyes are dark and always sad . . . I suppose because he's never satisfied, but I didn't know that then.

Just when I thought I'd have to leave because the suspense was too much, he asked me.

Want to . . . ? Something like that.

I've been waiting for you to ask, I said.

And then he smiled. Now, his teeth are perfect. They're just like teeth on male models in fashion mags and his gums are pale pink and he has a little black moustache and it's a fine line above his pink lips, and he's got a cleft in his chin and his jaw's dead straight across.

Oh God, did I fall for him!

We danced together but not touching and he was gazing down into my face.

I'm being posted tomorrow, he said.

I felt like he'd slapped me across the face.

He took me home and we stood outside my house. It was a real freezing night but my cheeks were burning. I remember looking up and seeing this sharp little slice of bright white moon, and thinking, I'll never, ever forget this, and I haven't, but for different reasons.

I'll write you, he said, and then he kissed me. That was the first time. I was panting like I'd been running a race, and he was too, and I opened my eyes and his face was real white and there was this thin moustache and his white teeth. All of him was just right, not a crease in his uniform or a hair straggling – he was perfect.

'Mam, Mam, can we buy some goodies?'

'No, Sheralee, we're going round to Mrs Johnson's and she'll have some bickies . . . just wait.'

'Want goodies.'

'No, Kelly, you heard what I said.'

By this time he'd driven off in the blue van. It was more like one of them vans they use to take bodies from hospitals to the undertakers.

I was in a strange mood; seeing him like that was bringing it all back.

He was gone for nearly two years and all that time we wrote every day. I'd be rushing back at night, pedalling on my bike fit to bust, because I had to open our front door and see his letter on the hall table. All day in Needlers, watching the toffees trickling along the belts, I'd have been dreaming of it. He always used to start, 'My own Darling', and finish, 'All my love'.

And I'd be sitting there eating the tea my mam had put in front of me, gobbling it down so's I could rush upstairs and sit on my own in my bedroom with his letter. Just the way his blue biro had formed the letters, always so neatly, could thrill me. I used to keep all these airmail letters in a box that I'd tied up with pink ribbon.

All my love, Dean . . .

'Mam, Mam, are we nearly there? . . . I'm tired.'

'Yes, Sheralee . . . that's Mrs Johnson's over there.'

Michelle came to the door. I could hear her kiddies squabbling in the back and her mam trying to quieten them down.

'Oh, Karen, fancy seeing you . . . Come in.'

She'd put on quite a bit of weight, like me I suppose, and

she'd gone blonde but needed her dark roots doing. I could see 'em when she bent down to talk to Kelly.

'It seems a long time,' I said.

'Yeah . . . years . . . Here, you two, go and play with Kimberly and Harry . . . leave us alone for a bit.'

They were clingy and shy, but when Mrs Johnson got the biscuit tin down, and the orange, they cleared off.

We went into the front room and sat on the settee before Mrs Johnson's coal-fire – it's one of them that looks like real coal but isn't, and there's a gas flame keeps leaping up and down in the black lumps.

Telly was showing these aircraft taking off and a chap was saying, 'Well, of course, these days we can pinpoint our missiles with tremendous accuracy . . .'

Then he talked a lot about the various planes and what they could do and behind him you could see these massive explosions.

'Barry'll have gone then?' I said.

'Oh yes . . . he's been out since Boxing Day.'

I felt a bit embarrassed and didn't know what to say.

'Eh, we had some good times, didn't we . . . ?' I said.

'Yer . . . Shall you have a martini, Karen, or would you like a gin and orange?'

'Martini, I should think, please – we used to be right old boozers, didn't we?'

'Yer . . .'

I watched Michelle lurching over the shag-pile carpet to this little corner bar that her mam and dad had. She was wearing real high stilettos and a short tight skirt and a big 'sloppy joe' sweater.

She'd poured us two whacking drinks. I didn't like to say I'd had to give up drinking like that – what with being on my own with five kiddies.

We looked at each other.

'Cheers!' she said and smiled.

She's a big girl and quite pretty, and when we were looking at each other it all came flooding back. We'd both been army wives – I'd married Dean the day he arrived back from overseas. The girls at work had said:

Karen, how can you marry him like that? You don't know him . . .

Oh, but I *do* . . . I've written to him every day for two years. I love him.

It was a white wedding. I was the virgin bride. Michelle got married about the same time.

We shared pregnancies, shared practically everything. No sooner had the men left than she'd be on the phone to me, or I'd phone her.

Kar . . . coming round tonight? Bring the kiddies . . . then you can stay over.

We'd bed all the kids down first and then we'd get the plonk out and one of us would fetch the take-aways in, and we'd sit there knocking back vino and watching videos until the early hours.

I'm glad to see the back of him, she'd say; and I'd say: Yes, the place isn't your own, is it, when they're there.

Then we'd have a good laugh about how they carried on at home and how they wanted to throw their weight about and never knew how to mend anything or do any DIY and weren't the least bit interested in the kids.

I knew all the most intimate details of their lives – that she'd decided on a coil after Kimberly, and how Barry couldn't abide anything to do with periods and she had to pretend they didn't happen, and how they did it twice a week when he came back and he had this thing about girlie mags, and then there was this kid she'd had an affair with . . .

It was different with me, though, because although I'd grumble about Dean and be glad to be shut of him, in one way there still used to be some sort of magic between us. When the letters would start arriving again, I'd forget about the bits that weren't right, or maybe I'd pretend they weren't there.

Anyway we got stuck into our drinks, and then she said,

'Have you been all right since . . . you know, Karen, since you split up?'

'Oh yer,' I said, 'haven't seen him for yonks, and then as I was coming here, guess who we walked into . . . HIM!'

'What did he say?'

'He didn't.'

'Oh . . . I never expected you to split up.'

'It was all right until he got invalided out . . . It turns out I didn't know him after all.'

'Is that right?' She took out her fags and lighter, offered me one. I shook my head and then she lit up. Her eyes were on the screen.

'Do you know, Kar, I've been sitting up watching this all last night. They've shot down two British planes and one Saudi and two US up to pres. But we've hit some vital installations . . . I could do with matchsticks to prop my eyelids open. The kiddies have been watching as well, though they got bored after a bit because nothing happens. My mam says they're all sitting up on the estate. Nobody's talking about anything else in the supermarket – well, I suppose it is a big event like, isn't it? Let's have another one, shall we?'

Before I could say a word, she'd glugged this drink into my glass again and was taking her own down in big gulps.

'Yes,' I went on, 'I hadn't a clue who he really was.'

She wasn't looking at me, just inhaling her cig and leaning back against the settee and poising her legs. She was showing a great chunk of thigh but she didn't seem to notice.

'He just carried on at home as if he was still in the army . . . you know, up on the dot . . . kids had to be dressed and ready, and if we ever had an appointment nobody dared be a minute late . . . I used to dread it.'

'Mm . . .'

'And he'd be running his finger along the window ledges and the mantelpiece . . . he called me a slut and then he gave me a black eye and loosened my teeth.'

'Oh yes.'

'When he'd finished with the army, that was him finished

. . . it was like his home. I couldn't bear having him around by the end.'

'Yer.'

She didn't seem interested for some reason. We watched this missile landing and a great bonfire of flame whooshed up. You could see the air shimmering. Then we had another couple of drinks.

'I don't mind it, you know, Kar, except that most of the time, I'll tell you honestly, it's boring . . . though it's been better lately, you know, since the war. Well, I mean to say, you kind of feel at last something's happening.'

I don't know whether it was the booze or having run into Dean again, or seeing Michelle, or the war, or a combination of all of them, but I was feeling as though I wanted to cry and cry . . .

'Pity you're not around any more,' she said then and looked at me, smiling, and I seemed to see the old Michelle there again and remembered all the laughs we'd had and the secrets we'd shared.

Never, ever tell Barry about Don, will you, Kar . . . not ever . . . Basically he's a lot better in bed than . . . but you know there's the kiddies and everything . . .

Secrets you'd keep inside you until you died. I'd been bound to her by all that. It was her who held my hand in the labour room first and second times . . . she heard me cursing and screaming . . . she knew what I was like when all the cover-ups were off . . . I could have confessed anything to her and her to me . . .

'Yes,' I said, 'I miss us . . . that was the best thing about those times.'

'You wonder where it'll all end, don't you?' she said suddenly.

It was a funny feeling, being in that room with her at her mam's – half of it seemed to be different, but then other bits 'ud keep coming through and I kept wondering if nothing was for real.

The phone in the hall started ringing and I suppose her

mam went to answer. This bloke on telly was talking about the war and saying that it wouldn't be over all that fast, and then the front-room door opened.

I'd turned to see who it was, thought it might be the kids. Mrs Johnson was standing in the doorway, and when I looked into her face I knew something dreadful had happened.

'It's Barry, love,' she said, straight out, 'he's been killed.'

'Oh, Kar,' Michelle groaned, and I put my arms round her. 'What was it?'

'Seemingly a tank overturned . . . it was that.'

'Dead . . . he's dead!' She began to howl then and it was awful.

'I'd best go and stop them kiddies coming in,' her mam said, 'we mustn't let them get upset.'

'Oh, I knew something 'ud happen . . . just knew it.' She was still crying and her nose was running. 'Kar, he won't ever come back.'

'No,' I said.

'It's over,' she said, 'just like that . . . finished.'

This guy was still talking about the missile capabilities, in this very reasonable voice.

I stopped holding on to Michelle, because it seemed embarrassing to carry on once the worst of the crying was over.

There'd been one night when she'd rung me very late on.

Kar, I'm in love with Don . . . I just think he's wonderful . . . I'm dreading Barry coming back . . . Barry's always that matter-of-fact – can't show emotion . . .

And even that had passed. By the time Barry returned, everything had been just the same, or nearly.

Whilst I was sitting there listening to Michelle talking, I started wondering about my gran and grandad – he'd been killed in the last war and my gran had this picture of an airman up on her mantelpiece. There was another in her bedroom as well . . . my grandad. I know loads of people who've lost their dads and grandads in wars. Suddenly I fell to thinking how it must have been: had all those women really loved those men – or could they say they did, just because they had that one picture? It was like the night I met Dean and we stood outside my mam and dad's and he kissed me . . . or like the day we got married, when I saw him at the church door and he seemed that perfect . . . but he hadn't been perfect really . . . or at least it was the perfect bits that had killed it in the end.

If it had stopped there, if that had been the picture, it would have been fine. I would have been happy mourning my whole life, because I had found real love. But it hadn't . . . it couldn't stop there – the pictures had to keep flickering on. What would all these marriages have been like if the men hadn't got killed?

'Oh, Kar, I don't know what to do,' Michelle said.

'It'll be a long time,' I said. I knew she'd have him in a silver photograph frame on the mantelpiece and there'd be another by her bedside, and it would be worse because she hadn't loved him. But perhaps in time she would forget she hadn't, or maybe she had already; and then I thought maybe you could change everything in the past just by thinking about it. I would have to keep Don a secret from Michelle too, because she wouldn't ever want to remember about him, or how could she keep Barry in that silver frame?

Whilst she was repeating over and over, 'Kar, he's dead . . . he won't ever come back . . . What shall I do?' I realized that we'd never, ever be friends like we used to be, because Michelle couldn't confide in me any longer, and I would never be able now to be honest with her.

Love Me Tender

IT WAS ONE OF THEM DAYS that start kind of cool with a mist, only you know that it's going to get real warm. We never had many days like that. Usually it was rain, rain, rain, and you sat in and watched videos until you were ready to scream if somebody opened the door.

Being the holidays, it was my mam's busy time – perms and everything. They all wanted their hair done for going away, so she was glad to get shut of me for the day.

'You and Ange can go as long as you behave . . . Catch the train back about six – you don't want to be no later or you'll end up here at turning-out time.'

'Yes, Mam . . . Ange and me aren't daft, you know.'

We'd never been allowed to go there on our own before. Ange was my best mate and it was the summer we left school. I'd just turned sixteen. My mam wanted me to be apprenticed hairdresser, and although I wasn't dead keen I knew I'd have to. Ange would be going on this pre-nursing course, which I wouldn't have minded either, though I can't bear the sight of blood and yuck.

Anyway, she stayed at my house overnight so's we could catch the eight-thirteen to Scarbro', and we hardly slept a wink. We'd spent ages deciding what to wear. I was in my white trousers, white T-shirt and my white boots, and she'd put on her pink outfit. She'd tongued my hair and I'd done hers.

It had taken us an hour to get ready, and my mam had banged on the bathroom door and our Sean had bellowed, 'Eh, come out of there, you lasses, I'm bursting for a pee!'

There were loads of kiddies with their mams and dads and

their red plassy buckets and spades on the train, and they would keep crawling about all over and the mams were growing a bit fed up. Crisp-bags were crackling and tabs snapping on Coke cans.

Then these lads were giving us the eye up, talking real loud.

'Go an' ask her then!' this spotty kid kept saying. 'Go on, ask her!'

Ange said to me, 'Don't take no notice . . . pretend you haven't seen 'em.'

I was thinking about my fringe and couldn't be bothered anyway. 'I just hope it won't be windy when we get there,' I said. I'd got my fringe gelled down because I didn't want anybody to see my spots. Whenever the wind blew, I never liked going out. One minute I felt as ugly as sin and the next I was the most sexy creature who ever lived. All the boys would fall at my feet. Mr Right would appear – though as I took a size seven shoe I always had serious worries about whether I'd be able to cram my big toe into the glass slipper. I suppose deep down I thought I was a cross between Cinderella and the Ugly Sisters.

At home we didn't talk about Mr Right. There was just me and my mam and my brother, Sean, who didn't count, and our three Yorkshire terriers, all bitches. My nana lived two doors up. Men were taboo in our household. My nana's husband, my grandad, had run off and my dad – who I never met – had disappeared. My mam had been trying to nail him for maintenance ever since.

I want him put away . . . he should be put away, she'd say. I'll not rest till he's behind bars.

It sounded like tidying up, as though he had to be cleaned up and put in a cupboard.

You just watch out, our Vicky, my mam used to trot out, they're only after one thing . . . yer, one thing.

At that time I thought the 'thing' must be your money, because that was what grandad and my mysterious dad seemed to have taken.

'Well,' Ange said, 'what shall we do when we get there?'

Ange was one of these real quiet girls and she did more or less what I said. She was very neat and shy and she used to worry about things like being late for lessons or getting a detention. Her mam had nerves and a smile that flashed on and off like crossing lights.

'Let's go on the beach . . . and there's the amusements . . .'

We'd brought our cossies but we were both at the stage where we'd rather have died than appear in public in them.

As soon as the train stopped, all the bairns were squealing and their mams and dads were bellowing. The rowdy kids lumbered off in front. We brushed the bits of crisp off our T-shirts and picked up our bags. It was the big adventure. I couldn't wait to see the sea.

It was like being at a Rovers match on a Saturday, everything vibrated with excitement. All this swarm of people spread out and then we were moving forward. By this time the sky was bright blue and the sun was blazing and there was no wind, thank goodness.

This sign said, 'To the Beach'.

'That's it, come on, Ange.'

At first there were all these shops like M & S and Saxone's and we kept stopping to have a look – not that we could have bought anything, but it gave you an idea of the styles. Then they started to change and there were little cafés with 'egg and chips' and 'beans on toast' written in white on the windows and these dark Italian and Indian restaurants and a smell of curry. We stopped for ages at this joke shop. It had some disgusting things: women's boobs; some Dracula teeth; a chamber-pot called Thunder-bird with an eye in the bottom; joke dog turds; false noses and great black tarantulas.

'Let's go an' have a look inside,' Ange said. She was scared but she wanted to see everything.

There were plastic bats with black slithery wings tethered to the ceiling, and gorillas and Frankenstein masks and witches' fingernails. Things kept bumping into your face. It was real creepy and there were all these skinheads wandering around, so we got out smartish.

After that we followed the road straight down. I could feel myself becoming more and more excited. And then there it was. The sea was dead in front of us – all blue and shimmery – and there was a fair with a big wheel and a loop-the-loop and roundabouts. A line of donkeys were lumbering along the sand with this gypsy man. Kids were knocking a ball about or digging sand castles while their mams and dads snored in deckchairs.

We could hardly wait to be down there.

'It's all right, isn't it?' I said to Ange.

'Yes,' she said, 'only I don't want to get any dirt on me trousers – that sand can muck you up.'

'Yes,' I said, but I was thinking how fantastic it was – better than anything. I was loving it. I wanted to go on the rides; see everything; do everything; eat everything. I could smell onions sizzling on the hot-dog stalls and chips frying and chunks of fish.

'I'm that hungry,' I said.

'We've our sandwiches to eat first,' Ange said. She never got carried away by anything. It was different with me.

'Oh, come on, let's have a bag of chips at least!'

So we did, and we walked along the prom eating golden brown chips out of paper bags. They were real scrunchy. All along the sands kids were playing. Some lads had their trunks on and I'd be wanting to stare but didn't like . . .

After the chips, I said, 'Come on, Ange, let's have a look at the fair . . . go on a few rides.'

Ange had started gobbling down her Twix and her Mars bar by then. She never stopped eating, did Ange, but she was practically as thin as this anorexic kid at school.

Before we went into the fair we popped into a toilet to check our make-up and spray our hair. My fringe was holding down a treat. I was thinking that if we went on the loop-the-loop or the big wheel it might make my fringe come flapping up.

We'd just passed the fortune teller's caravan when we saw this bingo stall. You could go and sit on a stool and join in. In the middle was this big teddy with pale brown paws and feet and a pale brown face that looked real cuddly, as though he was smiling at you. I could see his arms and legs were jointed as well. He wasn't one of them cheap jobs made all in one piece.

Now I've always loved teddies and soft toys – more than dolls even – and I've still got my collection, of course. I like the way you can hug them and stroke them and they aren't hard and nasty and they make you feel safe. There's no problem about loving them.

Well, I looked at this teddy and I thought: I want him. I must get him.

'Oo,' I said to Ange, '*he's* all right . . . I must win him.'

'Yes,' she said, 'he is a nice bear.'

This chap had been watching us. He was in charge of the bingo it seemed. He'd have been about twenty. His face was very tanned and he had this coarse, brassy yellow hair; but it was his eyes you looked at. They were very blue and excited. When he stared at me, I felt funny and my heart fluttered. He had a big gold hoop in one ear.

'Want to play, love?' he said.

I went red. Ange was hanging back behind me.

'All right,' I said, 'how much?'

There were all these old women with shopping-bags sitting there staring at the prizes in shiny plastic wrappers that were mounded up in the middle with the lights shining on them.

He took my money and I saw these little birds tattooed between his thumb and his first finger. Because he was only wearing a sleeveless T-shirt you could see this snake swarming up his thick curved arms, and his shoulders were real broad.

'Are you going to play?' I asked Ange.

'Oh no . . . I'll watch.'

She'd started on her mint imperials and was looking edgy. All under my arms was wet with excitement and I was hoping my new deodorant would stand up to it.

His voice was hot and creamy – the kind of voice some singers have. The numbers droned on, 'Two and two, twenty-two; one and one, legs eleven; two fat ladies, eighty-eight . . .'

He was joking these women along and he seemed to know how to handle them. Then all of a sudden, he came over to me and shouted, 'Young lady here's got it! Yes, young lady's won!'

He did it real fast, but I knew I hadn't won. My numbers were all different.

'It's the bear you was wantin', is it then, love?'

Before I knew what, he'd put this bear in my arms and he was staring straight into my eyes and I tingled all over and it seemed very hot. I could hear this music from the rides booming out:

It's you, it's you, it's you . . .

And in all this noise and the groaning and creaking of the machines, there only seemed to be him and me.

I was just turning away with the bear in my arms and Ange at the side of me, when this old cow like the wicked witch bellowed, 'That's not right – that's a cheat . . . I want to see the manager – him wot's in charge . . . where is he?'

The man made a little sign that we should clear off quick, so we did.

I couldn't get over it. I was hugging the bear so that his cellophane crackled.

Ange kept on saying, 'Oh dear, oh dear . . .'

I began to laugh, and I laughed and laughed until I was bent double and she had to laugh too.

'Bloody hell,' I said, 'bloody hell . . . fancy that . . . and that old cow!'

'Look,' Ange said, 'you'd best open it, there's a paper tucked inside.'

And there was this note. It said: Meet me at four behind the roundabouts, Kev.

I was that excited I didn't know what to do, and I rubbed my nose on the teddy and hugged him.

Ange said, 'Oh er . . . you'd best not meet him . . . you never know. Your mam and your nana wouldn't like it.'

'Go on,' I said. I was thinking about his blue eyes and the birds where his hands curved and his smile – because he'd smiled at me. His teeth were square and gappy and stained with cigarette. And he'd given me the teddy. Nothing like that had ever happened to me before and it took my breath away.

We went into the amusements and had a go on the machines and then we climbed down on to the beach, took off our shoes and had a paddle, but all the time I was cuddling my teddy and I kept thinking how I wished it 'ud be four o'clock. There was nothing in my head, only four o'clock. I watched the donkeys plodding along and dropping these brown blobs every so often and I felt sorry for them, but the sea was sparkly and these little kids were running in and out as though it was magic. It made me want to run about and sing as well and I did wish Ange wouldn't be so glum.

By about four some of the families had started to pack up and go, but wherever you stood you could see the big wheel circling and the lights shining and I thought: It's you, it's you, it's you . . .

'Well anyway, we'll have to be going home soon,' Ange said.

'Don't be daft – it's only ten to four.'

We wandered back down the beach but I kept thinking: What if I miss him? What if he's not there? What if that note was for somebody else?

Dead on four we were at the back of the roundabout. It was jam-packed full of kids sucking lollies and nipping bits of candy floss and biting into hot dogs, and you could smell oil from the machines and hear the whirring and throbbing.

At first I couldn't see him, and then he turned round and he was leaning up against this stall smoking a fag and staring at me. I went ever so red.

'So you've come,' he said.

'Yer, thanks for the teddy,' I said.

'Think nowt of it – want to go for an ice?'

He took us in this café that was painted all white and had green-and-white counters. This Italian feller brought me and Ange a fantastic ice with an umbrella on top. My spoon went down real deep and there was a lump of honey-coloured peach and a cherry and some chocolate ice in the glass, but I could hardly eat because he was opposite me and looking into my face.

'What's your name?' he asked.

'I'm Vicky and this here's my friend Ange.'

'Pleased to meet you,' Ange said and gave him one of them crossing-lights smiles, just like her mam's.

'You know I'm Kev . . . Want to go on a few rides then?'

'Oh yer.'

So after the ices we went back into the fairground. He was walking between us but he kept on turning to me. He was quite tall and wore these boots and ripped jeans and he kind of swaggered and he had a cross round his neck.

Well, he took me on the waltzers. Ange wouldn't come and so I gave her the bear to hold. She said she'd wait. Before the ride started I could see her staring at me and her face looked frightened.

It started slow at first and then went faster and faster and this feller came behind us and made ours whirl more than anybody else's. Kev had his arm round me and I fell against him. My stomach shot up and down and it was terrible. You could hear all the lasses screaming.

'Do you want to come with me then?' he said.

I heard his voice in all this whirling and screaming, when I couldn't see anything because I'd shut my eyes. He was holding my hand and I could feel his hard thigh. I'd never been so excited in my life.

'How do you mean?'

'Come away with me.'

While it was whizzing round I thought I'd die. It made you feel sick but excited as though anything could happen: the best, the worst.

I don't know him, I thought, don't know nothing about him. On the beach Ange had said: You're daft, Vick, dead daft – he's common, common as muck. Fellers like him live in caravans and they have loads of kids – they don't stay anywhere and they don't get washed. And he might be a rapist or a murderer . . .

And while the waltzer was whizzing round, I didn't care. I loved his yellow hair and his blue eyes and I was frightened to death of him.

When the waltzer came to rest, everything seemed to return to normal. He helped me out, and when his hand touched mine, I went all hot. It was a firm, hard hand.

Ange was standing there staring at me.

'It's getting late,' she said. 'Your mam said to catch the six o'clock train back.'

'Oh, it's not all that late.'

It was a quarter to six.

'You'll not catch that now,' he said. 'You couldn't get up that hill and right along in time.'

'Oh dear . . .' Ange looked as though she might start to cry.

'It won't matter, we can catch the eight o'clock.'

'But that's the last one.'

For another couple of hours we went on rides and toured the amusements, and I thought, maybe he didn't mean it – what he said on the waltzers. I was waiting all the time for him to say it again.

'Look, Vicky, we have to go back now.' Ange's voice was little and bossy, and I knew she wouldn't budge.

'Oh, all right,' I said.

It was then that he came right up close to me. 'You're beautiful,' he said. 'Will you come away with me then?'

'But you're with the fair,' I said.

'Not any more – got the sack today,' he said.

Shivers went all up my arms and I came out in goose-pimples – he'd lost his job for me.

'Oh, I'm real sorry – that was because of the bear –'

'Don't mind. Well?' he said.

I thought of the dogs at home – Bubbles, Tanya and Peakie – and my mam and nana and Sean and having to be a hair-dresser's apprentice and getting varicose veins with standing and always having to sweep up and blow-dry some woman's hair who's a right cow, and I wanted to say yes.

On the waltzers when it was spinning like mad, I'd thought it wouldn't be bad if you died like that – just bang in a flash. Why don't I just clear off with him now, tonight, and never ever go back?

What stopped me? I think it was maybe Ange's face. She was my best mate, wasn't she?

Anyway, I just said, 'Walk us up to the station, Kev, please – we have to get back.'

He did take us up to the station, and all the time I wanted to cry because I couldn't say goodbye to him. I thought I'd never live without him.

'You're a lovely girl, Vicky,' he said on the platform, and he kissed me then on the mouth. Ange had already got on the train.

'I'll never forget you,' I said – and I haven't.

When it's one of them days that starts cool and comes on hot I think about that Kevin. What if I'd have run off with him, instead of staying put and doing what my mam and nana expected? I've still got Honey, the bear, too – there's twenty bears in my bedroom, all for cuddles.

The funny thing is, though, Ange, who never wanted to take any kind of risk, went off the next year to the Costa Brava. Well, she never came back. She got stabbed to death by this feller who was trying to nick her handbag . . .

Well, at least with the bears you know you're safe . . .

The Loss

THE NATTILY DRESSED middle-aged man was hovering near the jams. At first Barbara thought he was simply a ditherer, and then she began to have her suspicions. But surely he couldn't be a thief . . . he didn't look like one – his clothes were too good and he had the narrow, horsy face which she associated with educated people.

She concentrated on a little old lady; they were notorious. The more vulnerable their exterior, the greater the likelihood of their being up to something. Why, she'd known shopping-bags with false bottoms . . .

Her gaze swept back to the rather distinguished-looking, grey-haired man in the tweed overcoat. He was slipping a jar of expensive preserve into his bag.

Barbara flushed. The hunt was on. Such moments caused her a certain exhilaration. Right from those early days when Bill Smethurst, the retired policeman, had trained her, she had looked on the job as a challenge. She was serving the general public. After all, shop-lifting was stealing . . . stealing! Why call it shop-lifting, she had always wondered, when it was outright theft?

The man was striding purposefully to the check-out. Barbara dodged round a display island of dog and cat food, narrowly missed a shopping-trolley, and caught up with him as he fitted his wire basket into a stack of others. He paid for a carton of plain yoghurt and a tub of low-fat margarine; no jam. Barbara was sweating now. She caught a close-up view of the man. His skin was greyish, and he had that swarthy, slightly foreign appearance which she had always found attractive . . . but she was registering the word *thief* . . . thief.

Whatever happened she must challenge him before he could get more than a couple of paces from the shop; earlier than that and he would try to make the excuse that he was really about to pay but had forgotten to do so.

'Er . . . excuse me . . . sir . . . I think you've got something in your bag that you haven't paid for.'

She was blocking his way. Five foot ten and tough; she fixed her sky-blue eyes on him; her hand rested on his arm . . . not clawingly, and yet with a heaviness which must imply menace.

'I beg your pardon?'

His polite, cultured voice shocked her. Perhaps she had made a mistake, like the time when a woman had fetched out a jar of mayonnaise to check its price against that of the mayonnaise sold in the store, and Barbara, seeing the hand returning the jar to the shopping-bag, had thought it stolen and had challenged the woman. How she had blushed at her mistake! Could this be a smiliar case? No, she decided. She had seen him deftly picking up the preserve and lowering it into the shopping-bag.

'You have not paid for the jam – may I see the contents of your shopping-bag?'

He gazed back at her. She noticed how a muscle near his mouth throbbed; otherwise his face was blank.

The moment of physically arraigning people was always curious; her hand touching them, strangers . . . but she had to. At times she caught herself pondering as her hand encountered Clifford's arm . . . Clifford, her husband. She could not work it out.

For a fraction of a second, which seemed to last for years, they faced each other in the morning street. Spring. Her hand still rested upon his arm. It seemed ridiculous. He had steady grey eyes like striped pebbles. A criminal, a thief.

'Well? Would you please mind returning to the store?'

This was the scary bit. He might try to resist. At times she had even had to chase youths and girls down several streets to catch them. She knew how to wrench arms up backs.

The man stared at her impassively. She watched the nerves

in his face jumping and was unsettled by it. He wasn't going to try any tricks, for he merely shrugged his shoulders. Together they re-entered the shop.

'Please come to the office.'

Before the manager and several assistants the man prepared to unzip his bag. Barbara waited, heart pounding. Why didn't he say something?

Still in silence he placed the margarine and the yoghurt on the desk. Standing beside him, she could see the jar of raspberry preserve. It was small and expensive.

'There!' she shrilled with excitement.

'May I see your receipt, sir?' the manager asked in the smooth, tricky voice he used when he knew he was about to expose a thief.

The man felt in his coat pocket and produced the small strip of white paper.

'There you are, only the two items. You haven't paid for this, I'm afraid.'

At that moment two policemen entered the office. They had been summoned the minute Barbara had left the shop in pursuit of the man.

As they took the man away, Barbara watched. Generally at such times she would find herself glowing with a pleasant sense of victory, because yet again right had triumphed and the forces of chaos had been driven back. This time she was somehow embarrassed, and when, at the door to the street, he turned and glanced back at her, she felt her cheeks growing hot.

'Why does a man like that thieve?' she asked the assistant manager, who was lingering near her. A small crowd was watching the man and the two police officers climbing into the police car.

'Nutter, I expect,' the young man responded in a languid voice. 'It gets a bit boring when they go like that.'

'Yes, yes,' she murmured, wondering if that was the reason why everything seemed unsatisfactory.

*

Life continued in the usual way with its crop of students thieving boxes of Black Magic for bets or because they had some weird political views or just for kicks. There were ancient ladies who pretended to be vague but really knew exactly what they were about in pushing the packets of bacon or chocolate digestives into their handbags. Some women tried to brazen it out by wheeling shopping-trolleys straight out of the store without halting at the check-outs. Then there were the well-dressed memopausal women who pleaded temporary insanity. She knew all the ruses and they flowed over her without ever moving her in any way. All jokers, they were – people who would stop at nothing in what they might try on.

The case came up in the magistrates' court along with countless others. Barbara swore by Almighty God and gave evidence. The man stared back at her as before. It was a strange, disturbing look. He declined to give any explanation for his actions and was fined and led away by the court usher.

All the way through the cases of the university student who had stolen a packet of Maltesers and the youth who had broken into a condom-vending machine, Barbara pondered over the man. Why had he done it?

That evening she went to the pub for a drink with Clifford, and as she put her hand on his arm to walk back in the early May twilight she had that peculiar sensation of pressing her fingers down on the arm of a stranger. She glanced then at the side of his face, hesitant, wondering who this might be. But then of course it was Clifford.

'That man got fined,' she said, 'the one with the preserve . . . forty pounds . . . seemed a bit steep . . .'

'What man?'

'Oh, it doesn't matter.'

A hot spell came on in mid-May, and on her Thursday afternoon off she went shopping in town, intending to buy a summer skirt, something a bit flowery and feminine. She always saw herself as a big, heavy, middle-aged woman in severe dark clothes, whereas she would have wanted to be little and fragile, able to wear thin gold chains and five-inch stiletto heels.

As she stood on the escalator in Debenhams, riding down and automatically letting her eyes stray over the store, searching keenly for wrongdoers, she saw him. He was standing near the bottom of the escalator and he smiled at her.

'Hello, beautiful day,' he said as she stepped off.

'Yes, isn't it?' She gave a bracing laugh and managed to hide the fact that she was quite shocked at the sight of him.

'Would you like to come into the café with me and we'll have tea?'

'Oh well, all right then, thanks.'

'You aren't on duty, evidently?' he asked, looking at her quizzically. It was an amused, appraising glance; a challenge, she thought.

'No, no, it's my afternoon off.' She was blushing. 'What are *you* doing then?' That was not the sort of question she should have asked, she realized.

'Just out for a stroll – the weather's so magnificent, isn't it?'

'Yes, I've been buying a skirt . . . you know, with it being warm.'

'What's it like?'

Strange question from a man, she thought. She eased a corner of the garment out of the bag. It was a brilliant riot of fringed cornflowers and scarlet poppies with black centres – even as she looked, she knew it was too exotic for her.

'That looks very colourful,' he smiled, 'the sort of thing I like.'

She sensed that he too had longings.

'Well, I did wonder if it was really *me*.'

She ate a maid-of-honour and drank her tea and they talked of holidays.

'I've always wanted to go somewhere real hot . . . hot and strange,' she confided, 'but it's generally either Benidorm or Bournemouth. Cliff can't stand anything too way-out. He'll only go to Benidorm because he knows he can get his pint and his fish and chips.'

He listened and smiled, and she felt she was saying too much, but he seemed really to want her to talk and that was a change; men mostly did the talking around her.

They parted outside the store and she glanced shyly at his pewter-coloured skin. In the strong sunlight she could see the dark shadow of the beard waiting to poke through.

'Thanks for the tea – that was very nice.'

'I hope you have your exotic holiday.'

'That's not very likely,' she laughed.

They walked away in opposite directions. She remembered her hand on his arm and his wide-open eyes looking at her. So that's that, she thought, and as she unlocked her own front door and began taking the beefburgers and chips from the freezer for Clifford's tea she felt oddly let down. It was as though she had expected something else from the encounter . . . but what?

The beefburgers spat and hissed under the grill and ice melted from the frozen peas so that the water peaked and fizzed in the saucepan. She looked round the kitchen, seeing the glitter of melamine units and stainless-steel taps and wooden-handled knives hanging in rows from hooks. A glare was reflected bleakly from everything. On her way to work that morning she had heard a group of children shouting, 'Store detective, store detective!'

Hate had throbbed in their voices, and they had gathered themselves up in a scutter, their feet donging as they shot round the corner.

When Clifford saw her skirt, he wrinkled up his face.

'You'll not wear that . . . goodness me . . . far too bright! What do you think you are, a teenager?'

It would be gritty sandwiches on the sands at Bournemouth, she predicted, thinking of great heat and a hard blue sky and emerald-green twining plants with aerial roots, and macaws with black laughter-lines marking chalk-white and shrill-red faces. Disappointment curdled in her. She did not tell Clifford of the tea-party.

June was a blazing month. Barbara felt restless and she

often eyed flimsy holiday tops and sinuous dresses with hot longing as she patrolled the store. Passing by the perfume counter she lusted after a French scent-spray.

All manner of longings moved in her. She suffered from migraines and attacks of irritability. It seemed a crazy month; she caught a total of twelve shop-lifters. The manager gave her a special bonus and drenched her with his oily smile.

'If you keep this up, Mrs Stuart, why, we might, er, think of a rise.'

On the last day of June, when the weather had suddenly changed and become cold and damp, something awful happened in the afternoon. She was prowling behind the perfumery, having just been through the Food Market, when she saw him. He was wearing a straw-coloured linen suit and was positioned before the jewellery counter.

Barbara's heart hopped and she sweated. She noticed the way his grey hair grew quite long and curled towards his collar.

The assistant was showing him some gold necklaces, very expensive ones made of heavy woven chains. A colleague attracted her attention for a second and she turned away to answer a query. In that moment the man removed a necklace from the velvet pad and slid it into his pocket.

Nonchalantly, without any show of haste, he wandered away, making for the exit.

Barbara felt sick as she strode after him, pushing through the crowds of women buying holiday gear.

It was easy to catch him; why didn't he run or dodge away? Why, it was almost as though he was waiting for her . . .

She didn't want to catch him. Should she let him go? For a second she hesitated behind him, but training and habit made her accost him.

On a dying autumn day he appeared in court and was sentenced to two years' imprisonment, and Barbara, just back from Bournemouth, hearing the sentence sat appalled. Their eyes met once across the court.

After a sleepless night she made Clifford's breakfast, prepared his packing-up, kissed him on the cheek and heard the door judder as he left for work. Then, in haste but quite methodically, she hauled the Benidorm flight bag from the top of the wardrobe and began to pack her clothes. Three jumpers, a pleated skirt, a couple of Tricel blouses, underwear, her nightdress, towel and make-up bag; did she need anything else? Her gaze fell on her unworn holiday purchase, the bright skirt which still hung in the wardrobe. She unhooked it from its hanger and placed it in the bag.

Should she leave Clifford a note? What about his tea? Well, he would be able to eat on until he had emptied the freezer.

As the Yale lock snapped to behind her and she set off down the street in the direction of the station, she took a deep breath. She knew that she would not be coming back.

Love's Coming of Age

IT HAD ALL STARTED when Irene went to see Mrs Harper, the clairvoyant, and she said, Mrs Watkins, you're going to meet someone, a dark stranger, and it'll change your life.

Irene studied her face in the mirror. After Mrs Harper's prediction she had had her hair bubble-permed so that it covered her head in wild candy-floss squiggles; she had become a blonde bombshell who wore blue or violet eye-shadow, and whose lips were a scarlet gash.

Well, she thought, I look like a paper bag that's been squeezed up and smoothed out again. Her eyes concertinaed and cracks ran from her nostrils to her lips and down the sides of her mouth.

She gave a careful smile and bared her Sterodent-white teeth. Oh, it would have to do, it just would . . .

Now she wondered what Derek was going to say to her. It was unusual for a son to issue a formal invitation to his mother.

As she examined herself in front of the full-length wardrobe mirror, she enjoyed the sight of her navy-blue stilettos and the blue and white spotted two-piece. She pinned a white carnation to her shoulder. A touch of luxury. The petals frilled against the shimmering blue and white silk.

Life had fallen into Before Mrs Harper and After Mrs Harper; two definite demarcations.

Before Mrs Harper she had been Alf's widow, the mother of four sons, and that seemed to have been going on for a long time, and had also been dominated by the shadow of Alf. Alf, Alf, Alf. She had married him at eighteen and he'd been ten years older. He had spirited her away with his salesman's talk.

I've got a real nice line in blouses . . . very fine. You'll see, nobody else has got one like this . . . Oh, what blue eyes you've got . . . mm . . .

He had had a way with ladies, and a case with shiny locks that his soft white fingers had snapped open and shut.

At one time they'd had four babies under five and they were poor, but Alf sold his way to affluence and a big posh car.

Underneath, though, he was a very bossy man.

You'll not go back there, he'd said when Mr Edwards, the manager of a newspaper shop where she'd had a weekend job, once ran her home in his car. No, that's the end of that!

So she'd worked on the ladies' lingerie section of a big store. As she'd handled the knickers and the slips and the bras and suspender belts she had dreamed. Young women with bright red mouths and expensive smells had tweaked at little strips of black lace and nylon and had held french knickers up against their thighs and giggled; elderly women had thrust 'Daniel Lambert' knickers and massive ugly white bras on to the counter. Their legs were tunnelled with thick blue veins and their backs humped. She had watched them all and had lovingly folded the black satin or ivory négligés in tissue-paper and slipped them into smart chocolate-coloured bags; she was almost swooning with longing.

Alf had to have his tea on the table whenever he appeared, and there must be no delay. If visitors came, he talked. She smiled; she'd been smiling all her life, just a nice sweet smile.

Occasionally she had thought of that Mr Edwards who had given her a lift home.

Alf's dying had been gradual and, as he had faded, so his irritability had deepened.

Don't hover, woman, don't hover . . . Where's my coffee . . . where is it? Don't take all day . . . what the hell are you messing about at?

And she was dithering at the electric kettle, willing it to boil faster, and in trying to progress at the double she had slopped coffee into the saucer. He had groaned with irritation.

Suddenly he had died and it had been as though her ballast

had been removed. Life lurched about her, peaking and troughing like a stormy sea.

When, one June day with temperatures in the upper seventies, she had been bumbling along by the shop windows, buttoned into her winter coat, she had bumped into her old friend Bea from the lingerie days.

Haven't seen you for a long while, Irene . . .

No, been widowed, you know . . . Alf . . . Alf. Can't seem to . . .

What had it all meant? She, who had never really found Alf a raver, had been waiting for his call:

Get the kettle on, Irene!

Irene, slip out and put me a couple of quid on Desert Orchid!

Irene, where's my pain tablets?

Irene, shut that blasted row off!

What you need is a visit to Mrs Harper, Bea said. And so they had gone there together, she and Bea, to Mrs Harper's home in the middle of a sprawling estate. That was the Before Mrs Harper time . . . and now . . .

Irene decided she would not clop along to the bus stop, no, she would meet Derek in style.

The White House, Mother, he had said, the White House at eight, just you and me. Sorry I can't fetch you . . . too busy.

She didn't care. She would sit in a taxi and dream.

The smell of the carnation was in her nostrils.

'Nice taxi you've got,' she said to the driver.

'Yes, love, I just wish them who uses it 'ud be a bit more partic'lar.'

'Yes,' she said, hearing the rumbling of bile which was reminiscent of Alf . . . but she wouldn't think of Alf. Why would Derek, her big boy Derek, want to have dinner alone with her in the town?

He was sitting in the lager-brown light of the bar in his navy-blue suit.

Very sharp, Irene thought, very sharp. She loved the look of young men in well-cut suits. Young men had hard bodies, tight buttocks and thighs, and aggressive shoulders, necks like pillars. She used to watch them following their girlfriends at a distance when she worked on lingerie. Knickers and suspender belts embarrassed them, but they wanted to look into that forbidden territory. Lingerie and women's handbags were the great unknown . . . at least that was what Oscar said . . . Oscar . . .

She tinkled across to Derek, smiling. He rose and looked at her in a certain way; it was as though she glimpsed Alf in that opaque gaze. It made her jumpy, like when Alf told her she would never work again with Mr Edwards:

You'll not go back there again . . .

The silence had been lumpy with fluttery, unpleasant things which banged about like large dark insects. She couldn't bear moths and flappy things.

'Hello, Mother,' Derek said, 'what would you like to drink?'

'A G and T,' she said, realizing that he expected her to choose a sherry.

'Oh, er . . . right, back in a minute.'

Irene sank into a plushy chair and arranged her legs so that she could enjoy her stilettos. Before Mrs Harper she had worn cuban heels and reach-me-downs. Derek wasn't broad enough in the shoulders, but she liked the squareness of his head.

'Here you are.'

'Thanks, love.'

They sipped a while in silence. She suspected he was gearing himself up to make a statement, and that caused her to twitter.

'How's your work, then, love?' He was something important in a building society, she knew. Anything concerning money was deeply meaningful, Alf had led her to believe. So now she assumed a serious face with just a hint of twittering about the mouth.

'Fine . . . fine. No problem. It was you I was wondering about.'

Oh dear, this was it then. It was the Mr Edwards thing all over again . . .

'Everything's just as usual, love . . . you know me.'

They were summoned to the dining room. In the red and gold velvet gloom they took their seats. Irene's heart was hopping. She sighed and relaxed slightly . . . might just as well be here as anywhere, she supposed.

She ordered an avocado packed with orangy-pink shrimps and frills of lettuce and glazed with mayonnaise. They drank hock from green-stemmed glasses. Lovely, she thought, and stopped bothering about Derek's pending speech.

'Now, Mother,' he said, 'I hope you're enjoying your dinner?'

By this time she was slicing up her fillet steak, french fries and asparagus tips and had her eye on a slice of Black Forest gateau.

'Scrumptious, Derek, a real nice meal.'

'Glad you're finding it so . . . I thought we ought to have a meal together . . . give us a chance to have a little natter . . . there isn't often the opportunity. I'm so busy, as you know . . . Well, I wanted to say . . .'

Irene raised her blue eyes to his and twinkled. Yes, he was quite a good-looker but she did prefer swarthy men to blondes . . .

'Mother . . . Leo and Emma saw you . . . You have been seen with . . .'

She noticed with interest how a pink colour surged up his neck and into his cheeks. Derek had always been a blusher.

'Seen, dear? Seen?'

'I myself saw you with a man.'

'Yes, dear . . . seen with a man?'

'Do try to make this easier for me, Mother.'

'My dear, I haven't a clue what you're trying to say.' It must be the wine, she thought: how else would she be able to look straight into his face and smile? With Alf, she would have been paralysed by embarrassment and guilt for the shadows of things not committed or even formulated.

'You have been seen all over the town with somebody half your age.'

She heard the horror and distaste in his voice. His cheeks were now brick-red.

'Mother, you must act your age . . . after all, you're seventy-three, not some teenager . . . Where is your dignity?'

Irene gave her biggest smile and her face shot into a thousand crinkles, her lips were a smudgy O. He was staring at her with real anger, she saw, and she couldn't stop laughing. She took a swallow of red wine, which had a smooth, dark taste, and spluttered a bit.

'Derek,' she said, 'what does it matter?'

'Mother, it's disgraceful. You're an old woman and he's a . . . he's a . . .'

'Yes?' she said. 'Yes?'

'Oh, a monster.'

She found herself laughing again until the tears stood in her eyes and other people turned to stare at their table and Derek aimed nervous glances about.

'I don't understand, Mother.'

'No,' she said, 'no, son, you wouldn't.'

How to tell him? How to tell the tale of Oscar, the sailor, long-distance lorry-driver, odd-jobber, who had a big gold hoop in his right ear and wore a black pin-striped suit and whose cheeks were blue and pitted and who smelt of cigarettes and musky aftershave?

You're a stunner, he told her that first night in the bar . . . a proper old stunner.

In that brown gloom with the red and purple disco lights flaying the little dance floor and everything on it so she'd thought of an epileptic fit, she had fallen in love for the first time in her life.

Mrs Harper had foretold it all: You're going to meet someone . . . a dark stranger who'll change your life.

The gel shone on his black hair, and his teeth bit on laughter.

Oh, you make me laugh, you old stunner, you do . . .

He and she stood on the pier at three-thirty watching the humping and weazling of the sea in the summer night.

You'll be out on that soon and I'll think of you . . . I'll think: He's away out there . . . my sailor.

Yeah, sailor, sailor with a girl in every port . . . you lovely old witchy bag.

And she had felt as though bits of her were streaming away on the still night air: she was part of the ribbed glossy water and the smell of salty sea life; the slubbing of waves on small craft and on the pier legs; she was part of him too – a man of forty-five who took her to the dog track and the races and drank with her in bars; she was also part of all those who had ever loved . . .

On that first night he said –

Can I take you home?

No, she said, no thank you. So he put her in a taxi.

And then he phoned; he started phoning, and she was forever dangling in a madness. It was ecstasy, it was hell.

He was a man who liked the life of bars and women's laughter, and he was always travelling.

Irene looked at her son across the table and she smiled. It wasn't her flickering, tinkly smile, from the years with his dad; it was a deep, secret smile, which halted him.

'You've no need to worry about me, Derek . . . It's nice of you to care though.'

He shifted his buttocks in discomfort.

'I'm only thinking of what people will say . . .'

'But why should that matter, lad?'

He didn't know what to make of her.

'Some time you might understand.'

He wanted to drive her home then but she said she'd be all right thank you very much and she had him call a taxi.

'Drive us to the pier, love,' she said to the driver. 'I'll just be a little while . . . Wait for us, please.'

And she donged along the wooden planking and went to stand at the rail. She watched the lovely juddering and winding of the water which was like a live presence and she thought of Oscar. The whole world was jostling with aliveness and such beauty that she could feel her heart bumping in her chest and she remembered that morning's interview with her doctor:

My dear, it could happen anywhere; you could go at any time. You should try to limit your activities.

That was her secret and she clutched it to her, like she did Oscar with his blue cheeks and the pink insides of his mouth and his body that was not quite a young man's and bore the traces of many foragings . . . and always the laughter . . .

Yes, she wanted to go with the laughter and the loving, launch out over the slapping and slithering of the waves in a big, soaring climax.

The Last Oasis

IT'S 'EARLY BIRDS'. The coldness in the air makes the women's nipples bud up and form hard dark blobs under their swimsuits. Vapour is twining above the water and the swimmers slide through it, appearing and disappearing.

Ed stands on the side and watches them. He watches the steam rising too. He loves this time: the frantic pedalling on his bike to be at the baths for 6.45; then the boiling mug of sweet tea and the first fag of the day with Tessa and Ricki. Her eyes'll be half closed and a bit puffy. In her navy-blue tracksuit, you'd never guess at the heavy swell of her lozenge-shaped thighs and the solidity of her back and shoulders. Her breasts are quite small but nicely shaped.

Here on the bath-side you might imagine you were out in some strange tropical world where the sea is a boiling vat. The great glass roof arches and the winter sun is behind it so that rosy light drenches the panes. Outside, the pavements dazzle with hard white rime and the road is covered with glistening scurf; the trees stand out in black twines on the white sky – you can never believe in that world once you're inside this grotto.

He's in a mood of subdued anticipation. It's Friday, the shift lasts until nine tonight – for the last part there'll only be him and Tessa and Ricki.

Ricki comes in then through the swing-doors. Ed sees the green rambling plants and the blue flowers in the leaded lights flash for a fraction of a second as the doors dong back into place. Something in Ricki's face isn't good news. Ricki's got thick white skin and strawy yellow hair and colourless eye-lashes. He's the sort of person who makes no impression but he's a mate, a blood-brother in a special way: one corner of the triangle base and he, Ed, is at the other.

'What's up?'

'Bloody Councillor Dingwall's coming on an inspection this aft. That's the fifth time this month . . . you bet sommat's brewing.'

Ed keeps his gaze on the scything arms, the hair sleek with water, the women's straining heads and prissy breast-stroke. He has an uneasy feeling in his gut.

Councillor Dingwall, chairman of Leisure Services, is a squat, pudgy man who has dreams of empire. Already he has consigned one Victorian swimming bath to Smythe's, the demolition contractors, and in its place the Dingwall Leisure Centre has been erected. Ed was transferred there for several weeks whilst his own bath was closed for maintenance.

The Dingwall Leisure Centre squats like a glassy superstore or an aircraft hangar amid lawns and concrete pathways. It is crammed with fiddle-faddle things: a wave-machine, kiddy pool, jacuzzis, gymnasiums. On the half-hour a voice screeches through the P.A. system and swimmers bumble to the shallow end as the assisted waves hump down the bath. He has stood, sweat draining along his armpits and bubbling on his forehead as the temperature soared to 110°F. It's a huge greenhouse with the heat sealed in and the humidity rotting the woodwork and corroding the metal . . .

Tiles crack and drop off the bath-sides. The bath has been open two years now. The Council are suing the architects . . . but it's a marvel, Dingwall insists – a modern pool. Kids swarm on the three-coloured balls at the shallow end, fall off and hit their heads, go under, have to be rescued . . .

Dingwall is all for short, modern pools – lots of glass, and plastic yuccas, and rubber plants in troughs. Nobody swims any more. They lounge in the navel-high water and fix their glazed stares on the roof as though they expect to see plastic macaws perching there.

Ed despises the Dingwall Leisure Centre. He loves this big red-brick place with its green onion domes. It's an Aladdin's cave, a magic theatre, and its plaque announces the laying of its foundation in 1896. Behind the half-glass doors in which the scarlet, spear-shaped tulips twine, there used to be lines of deep porcelain slipper-baths, each in its own cubicle. Years ago his mam and dad got bathed there after work, once a week. It was a treat, so they say, to come from the chilly back-to-backs and lie immersed up to the chin in steaming water.

He thinks about those slipper-baths now, as he patrols the bath-side. Ricki has positioned himself on the high seat that oversees the deep end. Recently workmen have appeared and begun breaking up the big porcelain shells.

Who gave you permission? he challenged.

Council, came back the grunted reply.

What for?

Dunno.

All that day he was uneasy and angry. They could hear the heavy slugging of sledge-hammers a corridor away. Now there is only one slipper-bath left. The swing-doors have been sealed off and the curly brass handles removed, likewise the door-plates. Vanished, just like that.

The morning passes in watching. Young girls emerge from bath-side cubicles. Their cut-away swimsuits show the clean cracks in their groins. Their legs are long and pale. Under the skin-tight suits their breasts bob. Their buttocks are pads of muscle or squiggy cushions. Some dive and their bodies describe a lovely arc. Others slide on their goggles, mess about adjusting them and climb down into the water. Up and down, up and down – they have a rhythmic thrust as they pass, moving in lines towards the deep end.

Youths show off and splat the water on to the pool-side in trying for clever dives, and then gouge troughs about them when they crawl up the bath with their torsos half out of the water.

The old champion comes. He's knocking seventy, short and wide of shoulder and chest. He gets in quietly and then begins his butterfly. His shoulders rise from the water, his arms spread. He's like some great bird. His feet flip. In five strokes he's at the top.

Ed always watches him. Each time he's hypnotized.

It's time for a break. Tessa strides up.

'Tea-time – I've boiled the kettle,' she says.

'Did you hear Dingwall's coming?'

'Yep.'

Her big blue eyes are wide open. They're usually smiling, but not today. They look at each other for a fraction of a second. Nobody would know what happens here. He can hardly believe it himself. There's Tessa: forty-seven, perhaps, to his thirty-one; one of those big, blonde women with solid symmetrical limbs, a powerful woman. At Staff Training she dives, loses her swimsuit and glides like some smooth seal underwater. He catches her, holds her. She is slippery with water, weightless. They're alone in the long slab of twitching pool.

He came to the baths after years of odd jobs, mostly out of doors – the last one a community programme cleaning tracks for British Rail, rooting amongst broken bottles and used condoms, chunks of brick, Coke tins and husks of take-away dishes, always freezing, always filthy. That's all part of history. He thinks of it only now and then, for a huge wedge of his life is invested here in this Aladdin's cave.

For ten minutes he tilts back in a plastic bucket-chair with his feet on the radiator in the attendants' room, inhales his fag and sips his coffee whilst he stares out through the window at the passers-by.

He and Tessa and Ricki are the old guard; they have been sent here because they are listed as 'trouble-makers'. They won't endure two hours' unbroken pool-watching like the young kids straight from school who man the likes of the Dingwall Leisure Centre. *They* don't know their rights and they're too afraid to complain. In tropical temperatures they pant and sweat in the big greenhouse and faint rather than speak out.

So, here they are, two men and Tessa and big Iris, who

works in the sauna at the back and does the massage. She shapes and slaps and kneads pink, steaming flesh and whistles garrulously through her teeth.

What is Dingwall going to say? There's a tension building up behind Ed's eyes like he gets during the school holidays when the pool rings and clangs with screaming and shouting and laughter.

Time's up. He must let Tessa get her break. He twists out his fag – cancerettes, they say, but he doesn't care. Out he goes into the foyer. His eyes follow the mosaic patterns on the tiled floor and then flick up to the turquoise wall tiles. He knows each twirl in the curly leaf patterns, just like he can see the scrolling on the balcony rails inside the bath, with his eyes closed.

Tessa is coming down the steps from the pool.

'Hello, lover,' she says.

'Hi.' He gives her a long look.

'My, oh my!'

He's seen her with her head thrown back, panting, and her eyes closed; he's wrestled with her in the old laundry where nobody goes.

And that first time when he saw Ricki leading her in there, his heart capered and he wanted to squeeze Ricki's throat, or drown him . . . but then they all three held hands – Tessa and Ricki and he: Ricki and he are Tessa's boys. Tessa is somehow like the building itself: full of surprises, passion, laughter, thighs that can crush and caress you and sandwich you securely. She's all sure and firm, but vintage.

'See you later,' he says softly.

She doesn't reply but turns round and their eyes meet. He re-enters the bath. Some of the old-timers wave to him. He knows them by name. They come every week, some even every day, cruising the bath, chatting, practising dives through each other's legs. All sorts come there: perverts who want to wrestle children; young chaps covered in navy-blue patterns, who writhe in each other's arms and try to throw their partners underwater so that he must blow his whistle or yell at them.

It's his turn on the observation chair. He climbs up and

relieves Ricki, who smiles and moves off to the position near the door.

As Ed sits there, he imagines how it must have been when they drained the bath and covered it for the winter so they could hold dances. His grandad saw Louis Armstrong play his trumpet at the baths – a trumpet solo in there! He can hear its hot, thrilling yowl. The amplification shudders in his ears. All that's sixty years ago. He's got a record, an old 78, of Louis's gravelly voice – his thick fudgy tones join Ella's rich brown ones – 'A Foggy Day in London Town'.

That's magic. And now it's afternoon and turning amber behind the glass roof panes. Two young guys vanish into the showers. There are hidden soapings in there, all manner of movements lubricated with the slide of sticky jism. He knows what happens; knows every nook and cranny of this place. He is familiar with all the cracks in the scum-channels, he's cleaned them. In the changing cabins kids stick chewing-gum on the door hinges. He discovers deposits of it, likewise graffiti: 'J.C. has a big cock'. 'I love Jason'. 'D.K. is a fart and smells'. 'KL =LP'.

Suddenly there's a movement behind the half-glass doors leading into the baths. He sees Ricki stiffen. It's the supervisor and Councillor Dingwall and a couple of other blokes. The big one in the waxed jacket is the City Engineer.

Dingwall's eyes are darting all over. He has a very red face. What a bastard, Ed thinks. His hands are trembling with fury and he wants to leap down from the chair. Why can't he see? Is he blind? How can anybody fail to feel it? It's four o'clock time and the sun is burnishing the whole bath. You could think of tropical forests and green plants with thick succulent leaves blistered with moisture, jade parrots at sunset. Once they switch on the electric lights the orange glow behind the glass will fade.

The light jerks on. All these glancing, beautiful things . . .

He climbs down from the chair and is replaced by a part-time attendant. Now he moves to the door. The group of men are about to leave. He hears Dingwall.

'Yes, that's what I said, Monday . . . it's all organized . . . you'll have to redeploy these people here . . . yes . . .'

Ed feels someone is strangling him. He can't breathe. How can this vandal do this?

He wants to shout abuse, but he doesn't. He remains standing a few feet away from Dingwall, staring at him. Dingwall, feeling his concentration, turns and meets Ed's eyes. He nods at Ed and his mouth smiles but his eyes are questioning. And then he's gone, through the swing-doors, down the steps, clattering across the blue and orange mosaic towards the front entrance.

'Well, you heard him,' the supervisor says, 'you heard him say it – Smythe's are moving in on Monday and you lot'll be going to the Dingwall of Watford Street, if they'll have you.'

Ed is bursting with defiance, but he holds it in. Must play the crafty game; let them think nobody's going to offer resistance. His head is whirling. The supervisor lumbers off to his office. They often don't see him during the full seven-hour shift, and that's all to the good. His eyrie is high upstairs under the roof and he remains there, spying out the land or struggling his way through heaps of paperwork that make his head sweat. Some say there's a ghost up there . . .

'Oh, I can't put up with this!' Tessa says.

It's nine and they've just closed up. The three of them are standing on the bath-side and before them the long blue oblong frills gently.

'It's the end, just like that . . .' Ricki mutters and his pale eyelashes sink. 'All over.'

'No,' Ed bursts out, 'no, it can't be . . . they can't destroy this place – it's been here eighty years and more . . . no, they can't.'

'But how can you stop 'em?' Ricki's shoulders sag.

Tessa doesn't say anything, she's watching Ed. For her, for all of them, he has to devise a plan.

'Well,' he says, putting his arms round both of them, 'come here on Monday morning and you'll see.'

He won't be drawn. They wind the pool-cover over. All the

time he is aware of the two of them, of the big echoing cavern where Louis played his trumpet and the couples smooched. There is the pressure of all those bodies caught in a moment of striving – whether for some ideal of fitness or to escape themselves, he doesn't know. And always there has been the love; the twining, snaking forms of it . . .

They stand in the foyer now: Tessa in a neat anorak, navy-blue skirt and court shoes – just any other middle-aged housewife going home to her husband and family; Ricki, a youngish father of three in a bomber jacket and 501s; and he, Ed. His twenty-one-year-old wife and baby will be waiting for him at home.

He watches the ordinariness of them as they chain the main doors and leave through the side entrance.

The supervisor's final words were: 'Don't forget, report at eight at the Dingwall Leisure Centre, then we'll see.'

Ed turns once outside the building in the freezing night and looks up at the sparkling onion domes – this is some Russian palace, and around it spread Arctic wastes . . . He doesn't see the tatty supermarket pocked with electric orange special-offer posters.

On Sunday night he can't sleep. Sara beside him wakes too. 'What is it, Ed?'she whispers.

'Nothing, lass, go to sleep.' He doesn't tell her anything about it and he leaves the house at 6.40 to bike to work.

There's an icy fog and he winds a football scarf round his face and across his mouth. He has stuffed as many T-shirts and sweaters on as he can accommodate under his parka.

The street is silent under its winking sodium lamps. She's still there . . . It has seemed to him that she might vanish in the night, onion domes and all . . . but no, she's there with her lovely mellow brick frontage and the shallow flight of steps leading to the half-glass doors which are filled with leaded lights.

He enters through the Vapour Baths side and leaves his bike there. Now through the echoing, white-tiled corridors he slips. He glances up at the turquoise tiling frieze and is comforted by the delicate twirls and twists. The foyer leaps into focus as he switches on the lights. He skids across the mosaic to the side door which will lead him up to the supervisor's room. He will sit in there and watch for the first Smythe demolition lorries to appear.

The supervisor's room smells of fags, and two tit calendars are pinned up on the wall. Ed lights a fag. His fingers are shaking. Milk-floats zoom by on the road, and cars with blazing head-lamps. He waits and smokes. It seems to him that he is not alone in there. He is surrounded by all those longing girls and the lads with their hair slapped back with Brylcreme, too shy to speak; and the voice of the trumpet solo; the bodies frantic for love . . . and all just touching the miraculous, just for a fraction of a second – so many secret places . . .

It's 7.55 before the first heavy plant arrives. They're going to rope off the pavements. A mobile crane comes swaying up the road like some nodding giraffe, and then there's the big donger. He's seen that at work. The great cast-iron ball thumps the side of a building so that it caves in and collapses, sinking in a haze of dust and rubble.

He puts out his fag, checks that he's got his pockets stuffed with sweets, and then opens the office window, climbs on to the table and eases himself out on to a parapet. Coldness claws at his face. He wriggles his way along. Way down below him people have noticed him.

He's looking for Tessa and Ricki. There they are, two tiny dots. They are waving. He has it in mind to try to climb to the onion domes.

People are shouting. Their voices are a blurred noise. He takes no notice.

When he next turns, he can see them all gathered in a group and their faces swim together.

Somebody is bellowing at him through a loud-hailer. Sea gulls rock past him and he gets a clear view of their hooked yellow beaks and pale reptilian eyes.

They're telling him he must come down. A group of police

are taking over. Smythe's workers' protective hats are bright yellow.

They can all yell and wave as much as they like, because he won't ever come down; he won't let the big donger begin.